T0128439

TRUE PERSEVERANCE

TRUE PERSEVERANCE

ANTHONY "MARSMAN" BROWN

WESTBOW
P R E S S®
A DIVISION OF THOMAS NELSON
& ZONDERVAN

WestBow Press books may be ordered through booksellers or by contacting:

WestBow Press
A Division of Thomas Nelson & Zondervan
1663 Liberty Drive
Bloomington, IN 47403
www.westbowpress.com
1 (866) 928-1240

Scripture taken from the King James Version of the Bible.

ISBN: 978-1-9736-5739-2 (sc)
ISBN: 978-1-9736-5738-5 (e)

Print information available on the last page.

WestBow Press rev. date: 3/18/2019

CONTENTS

CHAPTER 1   RUTH IS RAPED GOING HOME FROM CHURCH 1

CHAPTER 2   RUTH TAKEN TO POLICE STATION AND HOSPITAL 5

CHAPTER 3   RUTH MAKING NEWSPAPER HEADLINES 9

CHAPTER 4   RUTH DISCHARGED FROM HOSPITAL 13

CHAPTER 5   BIG SET BACK IN THE MAKING 19

CHAPTER 6   RUTH TRIED TO COMMIT SUICIDE .. 23

CHAPTER 7   RUTH AGREES TO ADOPTION OF BABY 27

CHAPTER 8   NOT AN EASY ROAD 31

CHAPTER 9   RUTH CHANGES HER MIND ABOUT ADOPTION 36

CHAPTER 10   RUTH HAS THE BABY 40

CHAPTER 11   UNCLE LEO SURPRISE VISITS 44

CHAPTER 12   RUTH FINALLY STARTS COLLEGE 50

CHAPTER 13   RUTH GRADUATES FROM COLLEGE 54

CHAPTER 14   MARK STARTS SCHOOL 62

CHAPTER 15   MARK STARTS COLLEGE 69

CHAPTER 16   INVITED TO HATE GROUP
              MEETING 73

CHAPTER 17   MARK ASKS ABOUT BIOLOGICAL
              FATHER 83

CHAPTER 18   JULIE MAKES DNA DISCOVERY 88

CHAPTER 19   POLICE INVESTIGATION
              REOPENED 95

CHAPTER 20   SENATOR ARRESTED AND
              CHARGED 102

CHAPTER 21   THE TRIAL OF THE CENTURY 111

CHAPTER 22   MARK MEETS GRANDMA
              BUCKRIDGE 145

YESTERDAY AND TOMORROW

TOMORROW IS THE FUTURE AND IT
TEACHES THE HISTORY OF YESTERDAY

SOMETIMES EVENTS OF YESTERDAY MIGHT
APPEAR IN OUR THOUGHTS OR DREAMS

HOWEVER, IS OUR CONSCIENCE
STRONG ENOUGH TO DEAL WITH
SOME ACTS OF YESTERDAY

IN A WORLD FILLED WITH PAIN,
GRIEF AND SORROW?

WE SHOULDN'T BE ASKING OURSELVES
WHY DID I DO THAT YESTERDAY

IT SHOULD BE WHAT SHOULD I DO
FOR A BETTER TOMORROW

SO LET'S TAKE THE POSITIVES OF
YESTERDAY INTO TOMORROW

AND LEAVE ALL THE NEGATIVES BEHIND

UNFORTUNATELY, IT IS HUMANLY
POSSIBLE TO FORGIVE AND NOT FORGET

BUT DON'T LET THE EVILS OF
YESTERDAY CAUSE YOU TO BE BITTER
AND REVENGEFUL TOMORROW

RISE ABOVE WORLD EXPECTATIONS BECAUSE
THE HEART OF MAN IS DECEITFUL AND
DESPERATELY WICKED, SAID THE BIBLE!

ALWAYS SHOW LOVE WHICH IS
PRICELESS AND BLAMELESS

WORK OVERTIME TO REMOVE HATE WHICH
IS THREATENING TO DESTROY HUMANITY

SEEK GOD'S GUIDANCE AT ALL TIMES

FOCUS! AND REMEMBER GOD
SEES EVERYTHING.

CHAPTER 1

RUTH IS RAPED GOING HOME FROM CHURCH

Her name is Ruth, she grew up in a small peaceful town to the north of Houston, Texas with her Christian parents who she loved and respected very much. She had one older brother named Al who was serving in the United States navy at the time. Her parents were humble, hardworking people who were members of the Baptist Church in the community and they raised Ruth and her brother to love and respect Christ Jesus the Messiah. Ruth's family didn't have much while growing up but what Christ Jesus provided for them. They were most grateful and appreciated all they had very much by always praying and giving thanks to Him.

The year was 1968 and Ruth had just turned eighteen years old. She would graduate from High school in about two months with very high hopes of attending College the next year when a cruel criminal act ruined her life.

One Thursday evening Ruth attended choir practice at her Church where they had a very good practice session. After choir practice she sat in Church and rapped with some of her friends on past and upcoming events. While talking, one friend, Candi asked, "Ruth, is there a special reason why you're so nicely dressed in a skirt outfit instead of your regular pants outfit?" The other friend in the group, Janet laughed and asked, "Is your date someone we know?" Ruth looked at them with disgust and said, "Why is that every time a girl dresses differently a man has to be involved in your minds? Us church sisters shouldn't be thinking like this!" "I didn't mean anything when I asked you that question, so why are you getting so defensive?" asked Candi. "What is it to you? Please mind your own business!" replied Ruth. After saying that Ruth walked away from them and sat with Julie her best friend and classmate at school and started a more constructive discussion. Ruth said to Julie, "Have you heard anything from any of the colleges that you applied to?" "No but if I don't hear anything by the end of next week I am going to call and make enquiries." said Julie. "I think I'm going to do the same thing too but I don't think anyone else who applied to colleges have heard anything because we would definitely have heard something." replied Ruth. "That's true." said Julie. "So before we leave tonight let's hold hands and pray about it because I would really love to go to Harvard," said Ruth. They held hands and prayed for a few minutes and then they decided to go home. When they were leaving Julie said to Ruth, "You need a lift home?" "No it's OK, it's just a fifteen-minute walk away and I wouldn't want to make your father go out of his way, thanks anyhow." said Ruth. "No he won't mind because the road is dark and lonely and you're by yourself" said Julie. "Oh please I do it all the time." said Ruth and started her walk home.

While Ruth was on her way home she had nothing to fear because the town she lived in was very quiet and mostly crime free. People would sometimes sleep with their doors open, that's how confident the citizens were. Ruth continued her walk on a street that was very quiet and lonely, humming the song that she just learned at choir practice. She was passing an old abandoned building which was surrounded by bushes when a strong man wearing a mask snuck up and grabbed her from behind. Ruth tried to free herself from his grip but he brandished a big knife held it at her throat and said, "One sound and you are dead!" She did not recognize his voice because he spoke through the mask so she complied with his order because she feared for her life. The man pulled her into the old abandoned building, tore off her clothes then threw her to the ground with the knife at her throat and then raped her. He pressed the knife so hard against her throat that Ruth could not move her head left or right without getting her neck cut. In a desperate bid to escape thinking that he was going to kill her, Ruth grabbed a sharp piece of wood that was lying beside her on the ground and stabbed him on the inner part of his left thigh. The pain made him drop the knife and hold on to the area that was stabbed. Ruth seized the opportunity and quickly pulled up her clothes and ran screaming for help. A woman who was driving on the road saw Ruth running and screaming stopped the car she was driving and said, "Get in quick!" Ruth quickly got into the car and the lady sped off with her. While driving the lady asked Ruth, "What's the matter? Why were you running and looking so terrified?" Ruth explained in a shameful way, "I was just raped." The lady said, "What! Who did this to you?" "I don't know he had on a mask, I don't even know if he was black, brown or blue!" Ruth said. "Calm down I am taking you to the police right now because I can't believe something like this could happen in our town" said the lady. Off she went to the police at full speed.

CHAPTER 2

RUTH TAKEN TO POLICE STATION AND HOSPITAL

When the woman arrived at the police station she told Ruth that her name was Dorothy and treated her as if she was her own daughter. When they were going in she held up Ruth under her arms and helped her to walk because Ruth was feeling very weak. "Come on don't give up now we have to get into the police station to report the matter" said the lady driver. "Oh! This feel so embarrassing" said Ruth. They went inside the police station and saw a female sergeant sitting at the front desk and reported the matter to her. She introduced herself as Sgt. Pugg and took Ruth and Dorothy inside a room and collected statements from them. Sgt. Pugg had to be quick with what she was doing because Ruth was starting to show a lot of distress from the ordeal so she called an ambulance to quickly take her to the hospital.

When Ruth arrived at the hospital to the emergency

section she was quickly taken to a room and given treatment by a doctor. All her clothes were taken by the Police, put in a bag and tagged as evidence for court when an arrest was made. Sgt. Pugg left the hospital and drove to Ruth's home to inform her parents about the matter. When Sgt. Pugg arrived at Ruth's home in a marked police vehicle she saw a man standing at the gate. She introduced herself to him saying, "Good night I'm Sgt. Pugg, are the parents of Ruth Reid in?" The man looked at Sgt. Pugg with a worried look on his face and said, "My name is Sam Reid, I'm Ruth's dad. Is everything OK? I am here looking out for her because she should have been home already from Church." Sgt. Pugg looked at Mr. Reid with a sad look on her face and softly said, "Your daughter Ruth is in the hospital." "Oh no, is she OK, what happened?" he asked. "Your daughter on her way home from Church was raped" she said. Just after she finished making her statement Ruth's mother came out after seeing the police car through the window and asked, "Please tell me everything is OK with Ruth?" "The sergeant said that Ruth is in the hospital" said Mr. Reid. "What happened, which hospital?" asked Ruth mother. "I'm sorry, she was raped and is at Main Street Hospital" said Sgt. Pugg. Ruth's mother took the news so bad that she broke down in tears and had to be hugged by her husband Sam. "Come let me give you a ride to the hospital" said Sgt. Pugg. "No thanks, I'll drive because we might spend the entire night" said Mr. Reid. Sgt. Pugg again expressed her sympathies and left them and drove to the scene of the crime where she continued her investigation.

When Sgt. Pugg. arrived at the scene of the crime the old abandoned house was cordoned off with police tape by officers who were already there collecting evidence. Blood samples were found by the officers on the floor which were left behind by the rapist, who was stabbed on the inner left thigh by Ruth. The rapist made his getaway and was not seen.

When Ruth's parents arrived at the hospital they saw her sleeping in a bed and quietly got two chairs and spent the night in the room with her. When Ruth woke up she saw her parents in the room with her she asked, "How long have you been here?" "That doesn't matter now, what truly matters now is, how are you feeling?" asked her mom. "Who did this to you?" asked her dad in an angry tone of voice. "I don't know," said Ruth. "You didn't even see his face or recognized his voice?" asked Ruth's dad. "He had on a mask and a long sleeve shirt so I wouldn't even know if he was black, white or blue. He spoke through the mask so I didn't recognize his voice." said Ruth. "Couldn't you at least scream and fight him?" asked her mom. "I wanted to but he took me by surprise from behind and he had a big sharp knife which he pressed against my throat. He was very strong and I was scared that he might kill me" said Ruth. "Don't worry the police assured us that they will work overtime to find out who did this to you and bring him to justice" said her dad. "Thank God it was not worse than this so please I know how you're feeling right now but God will pull you through" said mom. "This is the most embarrassed I've ever felt if an arrest is made I don't even know how I'm going to stand in court in front of all those people and testify" said Ruth. Just after

Ruth spoke the doctor walked in and asked her parents to wait outside so he could do his work.

Ruth's parents waited outside until the doctor finished doing what he was doing and when the doctor came out of the room he said, "You can go back inside now." Before they went back in Ruth's mom asked the doctor, "Did she get any sexually transmitted disease, did she get pregnant?" "So far according to tests done, there are no STDs but it's a bit early to know if she is pregnant but we are going to keep her under observation for a couple of days and when she is leaving we're going to give her some pills to take which should clean her out" said the doctor. "Thank you very much doctor," said mom.

CHAPTER 3

RUTH MAKING NEWSPAPER HEADLINES

The next day the news was in all the morning papers with words headlining, "Girl Raped Going Home from Church." Ruth was taking a walk in the hospital to stretch her legs when she saw one of the visitors reading a newspaper and happened to glance at the headline. She felt very hurt to know that something negative like this about her has gone national. Although the person reading the newspaper didn't recognize Ruth It was still a bitter pill to swallow, so she cut her walk short and went back to her hospital room. Ruth's admission in the hospital was a little longer than normal because they had to do several other tests on her to make sure she did not contract any sexually transmitted diseases but luckily she did not.

While at the hospital Ruth got several visits from her Pastor and other Church members including her best friend

Julie who said with tears in her eyes, "I am so sorry that this has happened to you but we are praying for you. Right now I'm feeling very guilty because I should have insisted that you take the ride home." "No you cannot blame yourself it's my fault I took things for granted living in an evil world where you should always be on your guard" said Ruth. "You know who did this to you?" asked Julie. "No that's the part that is worrying me the most because I might see him again and won't know it's him while he would be able to recognize me. You know, it's going to be very hard for me to trust any man again. Of all the evil things to happen in this world, why me?" said Ruth looking up and starting to cry. Julie sat beside her and hugged her while she was crying. Visiting time was now up so they held hands together, prayed and left.

That night there was a great thunderstorm and Ruth could sit in her room and see flashes of lightning through the windows with rain running down the window panes. While she was alone and feeling lonely in her hospital bed a soft spoken lady came to visit her and said, "Hi my name is Christine. I'm a patient in the room right across from you, how are you feeling today?" The lady was so warm and pleasant that Ruth didn't mind the visit so she started a conversation with her. "Not too good but I'm pulling through" said Ruth. "I saw when you came in the other night and you don't have to tell me I already know what happened" said Christine. "Wow! News certainly travels fast around here" said Ruth. "No, it did not travel fast but I know and don't you start worrying about that, it's cool" said Christine. "I've always read horror stories about women who had my experience but I never imagined that this could ever happen to me" said Ruth. "We have always underestimated the corrupt nature of man who instead of serving God they do nothing but try to be cruel and destroy themselves" said Christine. "I told my friend something similar a few hours ago that I should have been on my guard living in a sinful world" said Ruth. Christine rested her warm hands on Ruth's forehead and said, "Ruth do not let this set you back you're blessed, look ahead and achieve your goals in life." Christine removed her hands from Ruth forehead after making the statement and Ruth said, "Thanks I really appreciated those kind words of comfort." When Ruth finished speaking she did not hear any answer from Christine all she heard was the sound of rolling thunder coming from outside the window so she looked around the room and saw no one. Ruth was now wondering where Christine went and started shouting, "Christine, Christine where are you?" There was no answer and two nurses who heard Ruth calling Christine came running into the room and one of them asked, "Are you OK, why are you calling Christine?" "I must have been dreaming a lady came into the room a few minutes ago and introduced herself as Christine from the room across from this one. I spoke to her and then she disappeared" said Ruth. The nurses who were astonished looked at each other and one of them said, "Anyone leaving or entering your room we would have seen them and there is no room across from this one." "As far as I know, there is no one here by the name Christine so it must have been a dream" said the other nurse. "I'm sorry but I still don't believe this it seems so real and Christine knew everything," said Ruth.

The nurses tucked Ruth in bed while she was talking turned off the light and said, "Good night sweet dreams." Ruth laid on her bed in the dark and said to herself, "It doesn't seem as if any of the nurses believed what I told them, I know it was real and I have to be careful not to say anything about this because people might think I'm crazy."

CHAPTER 4

RUTH DISCHARGED FROM HOSPITAL

After spending three days in the hospital Ruth was discharged and taken home by her parents. She left with medication and was instructed to take one every day until finished. While on their way home Ruth was very quiet and her parents knew how she felt so they kept their silence by not saying anything either and only making their presence felt. However, Ruth's mom could barely keep her composure because tears rolled from her eyes down her cheeks the entire journey home. When they arrived home Ruth was warmly greeted by her Church brothers and sisters who were there waiting on her arrival. "Welcome home Ruth" said Julie her best friend. "Thanks" replied Ruth who was still showing feelings of embarrassment for what had happened to her.

Everyone tried to start a conversation with Ruth but she was feeling so down that she barely said a word to anyone.

The Pastor who was there prayed giving God thanks for sparing Ruth's life during the past few days and they sang songs together. While everyone was sitting in the living room the pastor took Ruth's parents outside the house where he could speak to them in private and said, "When we're gone please check on her as often as possible, cook only her favorite meals and try to be patient as much as possible. It's important that you do this because she looks as if she is on the border line of a mental breakdown." "Ok pastor," replied Ruth's mom and her father who lost the ability to smile since the incident only nodded his head.

The following day when it was time for Ruth to take her medication she couldn't find it. She looked everywhere so she came to the conclusion that the small bottle of pills must have gotten lost somewhere between the hospital and home. Because she placed herself in isolation from everyone she kept it to herself and didn't say anything to anyone that her medication was lost because her period had just started that morning. She was told that those pills were for that reason so she felt relieved that she should not be pregnant so she closed that chapter and went on with her life.

About a month after Ruth's discharge from the hospital her parents still kept checking on her as often as they could and making sure that she got only her favorite meals to eat. Ruth also got regular visits from Julie and other Church members who did their best not to mention anything about her incident. Ruth started to lighten up more and more to the extent that she started to show a smile and started to communicate more with everyone she was used to.

One day Sgt. Pugg the investigating officer came to visit Ruth at her home and saw Ruth sitting on the verandah by herself. Sgt. Pugg came out of the police vehicle and said, "Hi how are you?" "Words can't describe how low I feel right now" said Ruth. "You feel like you can talk right now? If not, I can come back another time" said Sgt. Pugg. "It's OK you can come and sit in the chair beside me" said Ruth. The Sgt. sat down beside her and said, "Good is there anything that you can remember, anything at all because sometimes there are things that you may think are not important but might turn out to be very important in the investigation." "The only thing I can remember is that he was wearing an expensive cologne, he was very strong I could actually feel his strength when he held me down," said Ruth. "This case is going to be a very difficult one not even fingerprints were found at the scene" said Sgt. Pugg. "Remember I told you that I stabbed him on the inner part of his left thigh with a piece of wood? At least a scar should be there" said Ruth. "There are thousands of strong males out there the police just can't go out and tell everyone to drop their pants to see their thigh but I'll make a note of it because that is important" said Sgt Pugg. At the same time Ruth's mother came out on the verandah and joined the discussion and asked, "Sgt. Can I offer you something to drink?" "No thanks I was just leaving but from time to time I will stop by. Anything you remember Ruth call me" said Sgt. Pugg.

One day while Ruth and her mother were alone at home sitting in the living room conversing her mom was telling her about herself while growing up in Jackson, Mississippi how tough it was in those days for people to move around and get jobs. She told Ruth that farming was the main source of income and you had to walk long distances to get where you wanted to go. She told Ruth that her father's side of the family lived about two miles from where she grew up and they too were also poor because his family was very big. When her mother finished talking Ruth asked her, "Do you or dad still have any family living in Jackson, Mississippi after all these years?" "After my parents died my only brother moved to New York to work and is still living there. I got a letter from him last week saying everything was OK and he is hoping to see me soon because it has been quite a while. While your father's brothers and sisters are living all over the States because of employment opportunities, I think you should sit and ask him about them he should be able to tell you more" said her mom. "Dad told me once that his parents died when I was a baby but he has not seen any of his brothers or sisters for over ten years now" said Ruth. "This scattering of families was because of the economic situation, people have to go and live where they can find jobs to survive and raise their families" said mom. "When I graduate college and start working I'm going to plan a family reunion and bring the family together because I assume I have a lot of cousins that I have never met" said Ruth. "That would be very good and let's pray that everyone is in good health," said mom. "Speaking of health, what kind of family illnesses run in our family? Because every family has an illness that passes down from generation to generations" said Ruth. "I can't tell you much about your father's side of family it would be best if you ask him but they were very stubborn. On my side of family my mother had a heart problem but she still managed to die from old age and I can't remember ever seeing my father being sick before he died" said mom. "Well from the sound of things it seems like I've nothing to worry about but let's pray that none of my female cousins don't have to face anything like what I did" said Ruth. While the conversation was on health Ruth's mother asked her, "Did you take your medication until they were finished?" "No I did not take them because I could not find them" replied Ruth. "What! When did you stop?" asked mom. "I did not take any because they could not be found when I came home from the hospital but I am not worrying because my period has just started again for the second time since I've being discharged" said Ruth. "Oh my you should have said something!" said mom. "Stop worrying mom I'm feeling much stronger without the pills" said Ruth. "I can't help but worry because a woman's body can be very deceptive and you are very inexperienced but let's pray that everything is OK," said mom.

Meanwhile Ruth and her mom were at home talking her father was at his work place doing his maintenance work when a bulb fell from him and broke. Ron his supervisor and good friend who witnessed what happened said, "Woah Sam that's the third one you broke since this morning! What's happening to you today?" "I don't know I just can't concentrate but I'll pay for the damages." replied Sam. "No it's ok I couldn't ask you to pay for damages when you're such a good worker but you have to be careful because it could be something of great value" said Ron. "Ever since the incident with my daughter I can't sleep, I don't have any appetite and I don't even feel like speaking to anyone. I only communicate with you because we have been working together for such a long time and been through so much" said Sam. "You want to take a few days off to straighten up your mind? Because if it was my daughter I think I would have felt the same way" said Ron. "I'll just take the rest of today off and try to get some sleep and be back in the morning," said Sam. "Good, no problem I'll cover for you the rest of the day" said Ron. "Thanks Ron you're a true friend" said Sam who finished up and went home.

CHAPTER 5

BIG SET BACK IN THE MAKING

The following week Ruth got an acceptance letter from the college she applied to study to become a pharmacist. Julie also got her acceptance letter to be a lab technician. Both girls were very good in science subjects in high school so their main focus of studies in college would be continued in the sciences. A special get together was held at the Church celebrating their disciplined hard work and success over the years. Dorothy the lady who helped Ruth to the police station the night of the incident was also present at the celebration and that was the first time Ruth's parents had a chance to tell her thanks for saving their daughter. When Dorothy sat and spoke to Ruth's mom they tried their best not to bring up the incident with Ruth because this was the first time she'd been this happy since the incident. Dorothy asked mom, "Does Ruth have any brothers or sisters?" "Yes she has an older brother who is presently serving in the Navy" said mom. "Oh that's wonderful! It's really good when young people can step up and serve their country" said Dorothy. "He told me when he was about ten years old that he was going to join the army when he grows up and his wish was granted" said mom. "Wonderful it's really a good feeling when you have children making early wishes and seeing them come through" said Dorothy. "I'm not too sure of that because I miss him every day and now Ruth is almost on her way to College" said mom. "One side of you is happy and the other side is sad because you watch them grow up and then you have to let go. Not everybody can deal with that" said Dorothy. "True, come on let me take you around and introduce you to the other Church members" said mom.

With a few weeks to go before the start of school a lot of ups and downs were taking place in preparation for the start and everyone was excited. Ruth was at home one morning ironing some clothes on the iron board when she suddenly developed an upset stomach and vomited all over. Her mom saw what happened and said, "This is the second time in three days this has happened to you. What's happening? I think you should see a doctor" "I think so too because I'm having problems sleeping at nights feeling distressed" said Ruth. Everyone at that time only suspected an upset stomach so Ruth and her mother got dressed quickly and headed to see the doctor because Ruth's dad was at work at the time.

When Ruth and her mother arrived at the doctor's they sat in the waiting area and waited their turn. When it was Ruth's turn to see the doctor he listened to her complaints and asked mom to wait outside while he examined Ruth in the examination room. About twenty-five minutes after Ruth was examined the doctor came out of the examination room and invited mom back into the room to speak to both of them at the same time. The doctor said to Ruth in front of her mom, "Ruth you are four months pregnant." "What! That's impossible I've not being having sex! I have my period every month!" exclaimed Ruth. "Doctor, are you sure you're not making a mistake?" asked mom. "All the symptoms that she has and tests that I've done prove that she's pregnant. Ruth, you mentioned about having your monthly period, I want you to know that there are rare cases with women who still get their period and are still pregnant. So don't be fooled" said the doctor. Ruth's mom started to tell the doctor about the rape that had happened to Ruth four months prior when Ruth broke down in tears and said, "My life is ruined I won't be able to go to college, this can't be!" "I'm sorry to hear this but you can come back next week when another doctor will be on duty and get a second opinion" said the doctor. "I'll definitely come back next week because I cannot accept this!" said Ruth who angrily left the doctor with her mom and headed back home.

On their way home Ruth saw one of her high school friends, Michelle, walking in the opposite direction. When she saw Ruth she said, "Ruth I'm glad to see you, my family will be putting on a special get together for me this weekend because I will be the first one in the family to attend college. They promised to have lots of food and you are invited. If you see any of our friends from school tell them that they are specially invited too." Ruth just stood there with a serious look on her face not saying a word when Michelle asked her, "What's the matter why you're looking so sad, are you OK?" Before Michelle could finish her statement Ruth broke down in tears and her mom had to console her. Michelle now feeling sad asked, "Did I say or do something wrong?" "No you didn't say nor did anything wrong we just got some sad news a few minutes ago that we can't share with you right now" said mom. "OK Ruth I will come and visit you tomorrow if it's OK with you" said Michelle. "That will be fine, maybe tomorrow she will be in a better mood to talk" said mom. They said good bye and continued their journey home.

CHAPTER 6

RUTH TRIED TO COMMIT SUICIDE

When they arrived home Ruth ran into the house and locked herself in her room feeling very depressed. Ruth's mom tried her best to communicate with her because she knew the situation was very serious and didn't know the extent to which Ruth would take it so mom kept knocking on the door shouting, "Ruth, Ruth please answer me!" With all the banging on the door from mom there was no answer from Ruth so mom got suspicious and tried her best to open the door but just couldn't. Mom held her composure and ran outside the house to get whatever help she could. Just as mom opened the front door she saw Ruth's father pulling his van in the drive way. Mom ran up to the van before he could stop properly and told him what was happening. Dad jumped out of the van when he heard the situation and rushed inside the house and took his crowbar from his toolkit and forced Ruth's room door open.

When the door opened Ruth parents rushed in and saw her lying on her back on the bed with a plastic bag wrapped around her entire head. Dad quickly tore off the plastic bag from Ruth's head and as he was doing that mom called the emergency number for help. Ruth was lying motionless on the bed and not responding to her dad shouting while shaking her head, "Ruth! Ruth! Wake up!" Being trained in first aid techniques when dad saw that she did not respond to him he tilted her head back, held her nostrils and administered CPR. After about five blows in her mouth Ruth started to respond by moving her head and gasping for her breath but still struggling. At the same time an ambulance siren was heard pulling up at their house and mom rushed out and led the emergency team inside.

When the paramedics came in the house they introduced themselves and took over the situation by putting Ruth on a stretcher and giving her oxygen. They carried Ruth on the stretcher and then put her in the ambulance before rushing her off to the hospital. While the ambulance was on its way Ruth's parents followed behind in dad's van and on their way dad asked mom, "Why was my daughter trying to kill herself?" "While we were at home today Ruth felt sick so I took her to the doctor and the doctor examined her and told her she was four months pregnant" said mom. "What! But how could this be she told me she had her period" said dad. "Yes that's true she had her period but the doctor explained to her that there are rare cases where a woman can have her period and still be pregnant. And that was what triggered the suicide attempt when she started to think about her college setback" said mom. "She looked as if she took it very hard because that was a gruesome way to try to kill oneself" said dad. Just as he finished speaking the ambulance arrived at the hospital.

When Ruth's parents parked and went inside the hospital building, Ruth was rushed to an emergency ward where a doctor asked them what happened. Ruth's mom in tears explained everything to the doctor including the pregnancy. Immediately the doctor went back to work knowing now the safest way to deal with the situation while Ruth's parents waited in the waiting area.

After waiting patiently in the waiting area for a few hours the doctor came to Ruth's parents and said, "I'm Dr. Wesley, your daughter will be OK. Her system collapsed when she could not get any air so we are going to keep her under observation for a while. The baby is also OK." The statement about the baby made Ruth's father furious but he managed to control himself. "Why are you so angry? I brought good news?" asked the doctor. Ruth's parents kept their silence to the doctor about how the baby came about but mom said, "It's a long sad story doctor." "You want to come into my office and talk about it? I have some time" said the doctor. "It's Ok," said mom. "Well if you change your mind you know where to find me because when you talk it helps to release the anger stored inside you" said the doctor. "Not right now but we really appreciate your help" said mom. "OK," said the doctor and went back to work.

Ruth's parents now feeling very sad and concerned as to what was happening to their daughter as she lay in a hospital bed for the second time in a short period, they started their journey home. On their way home mom said to dad with tears in her eyes, "Where do we go from here?" "I don't know, you tell me!" said dad. "Please don't answer me like that because this thing with our daughter is creating havoc in our lives, we almost lost her!" said mom. "You know that I have totally committed myself to Christ the Messiah so I'm going to go to him in prayer and ask for solutions to this problem," said dad. "I totally agree with that and let's do that as soon as we get home" said mom. They continued their journey home feeling sad but confident that Christ the Messiah will solve the problem.

CHAPTER 7

RUTH AGREES TO ADOPTION OF BABY

The following day when Ruth was allowed visitors by the hospital, the pastor of her church who heard what happened visited her and asked, "How are you feeling today?" "I don't think I can live with this. My whole life is ruined and I'm upset with my parents who should've allowed me to die!" yelled Ruth. "Don't take it so hard Ruth your parents love you that's why they saved you. This is not the end of the world there are a lot of trials and tribulation we are going to face in life but as Christians we have Christ the Messiah to comfort us once we trust in Him" said the pastor. "This pregnancy is my fault I should have said something when I couldn't find those pills now on top of that I'm going to pay a serious price" said Ruth. "We all make mistakes so as a pastor my word to you is to give up the baby for adoption when it is born and continue with college next year. You will still be young with the whole world ahead of you" said the pastor. "It's easier said than done pastor all my friends are going to be ahead of me and I hope that I can still do something about this" said Ruth pointing to her belly. "Ruth I hope you're not thinking what I think you're thinking please remember that two wrongs cannot make a right and as Christians we can only do what is right. Your pregnancy is halfway there so just hold on a little longer and it will soon be over" said the pastor. Ruth who had never raised her voice to the pastor in her entire life looked at him and said, "Pastor, you're talking about five more months and it's unwanted! This baby came about in the most horrific circumstances! Would you really want something like this for your own daughter?" The pastor stood there and looked in Ruth's eyes and saw her pain and looked away and said, "Sorry if I offended you with my words of advice, whatever you decide to do remember God is watching." After the pastor finished his last statement Ruth just lay there staring at the ceiling and said nothing more. The pastor said a word of prayer and promised to visit her as often as he could and left.

Shortly after the pastor left, Ruth's parents came to visit her looking very tired as if they had not slept in a long time. While her father stood silent her mom asked, "Hi, How are you feeling today?" Ruth took a while to answer then broke her silence and said, "I'm in a lot of pain mom, had you just let me die I would not be in this distress today." Ruth's mom sat beside her on the bed, hugged her and said, "We love you too much to allow that and we too are in distress. We spoke to pastor and he told us that he will help us to find someone to adopt the baby but it will be up to you." "Why would it be up to me? I don't want it and he already knows!" said Ruth. "OK, then adoption is the way to go. But you just have to hang in there till it's all over," said mom who whispered the adoption word so that dad would not hear. "I'm not too sure about the hang in there situation," replied Ruth.

Ruth's parents stayed with her until visiting time was up then they left and promised to return the next day. When they left Ruth was all alone on her back in the hospital bed with her thoughts. The nurses who would check on her from time to time tried to start conversations with her but were never successful. On one of their visit one of the nurses said to the other with a concerned look in her eyes, "I don't like the look in her eyes, I think we should start checking on her more often I just have a feeling she's up to something." "You're right because I really don't want anything serious to happen on my watch, it won't look good on our records," said the other nurse.

When the nurses were out of the room and Ruth was alone lying in bed on her side she felt someone touched her on her shoulder. When Ruth turned around to see who touched her she saw Christine her dear friend telling her to keep quiet. Ruth so happy to see her said, "Christine where have you been? Where did you come from?" "I've always been here observing everything that is taking place" said Christine. "Are you my guardian angel because you speak with so much wisdom?" asked Ruth. "Something of the sort but that's cool" said Christine. "I couldn't tell anyone about you because when I told the nurses they behaved as if I was crazy" said Ruth.

"I had to come and visit you again because I was getting very concerned with what is happening with you" said Christine. "I can't help the way I feel my whole life is ruined because of this pregnancy. What should I do Christine?" said Ruth. "The pastor was perfectly right, two wrongs cannot make right and you in turn will have to stop behaving like there's no tomorrow" said Christine. "This is not fair Christine. Why me?" said Ruth. "A lot of people ask themselves the same question but I have no answer to that, that's bigger than me. I'm going to give you a little history, thousands of women in this world who committed abortion in the past never got pregnant again no matter how hard they try. You are carrying a life which is very precious. Regardless of how it came about you have to respect that life and remember that baby is not responsible to be there. Do not fall into the group of women who took judgment on their own hands. God sees everything and you may not like the end results if you make that mistake" said Christine. Ruth quietly sat down on the bed and listened to her wise words of wisdom before she responded, "This is tough but I really don't want to fall out of favor with God" said Ruth. Christine held her hand and said, "You won't, just do the right thing and blessings will flow upon you. If only you know how God loves you." Before Ruth could respond she disappeared. "Christine, Christine!" shouted Ruth. One of the nurses on duty came running into the room asking, "What's the matter, who's Christine?" "I'm sorry I was just dreaming" said Ruth who didn't see the sense in telling her about Christine and went to bed.

CHAPTER 8

NOT AN EASY ROAD

Ruth spent one full week in the hospital but this time she was under suicide watch. She got several daily visits from her parents and church members as they too were very caring and concerned. During the days when Ruth was alone she realized how much her parents and church members loved her but her main focus was the baby growing inside her.

Another day while in the hospital Ruth got a visit from Sgt. Pugg the investigating officer who heard the news of her attempted suicide. When Sgt. Pugg saw Ruth lying on the hospital bed she said softly, "How are you?" Ruth took about one minute before she answered and said, "Have you made an arrest as yet?" "No not as yet but we are working very hard without success" said Sgt. Pugg. "This is not fair to me, my life is ruined and the person who did this to me is somewhere out there maybe enjoying himself!" said Ruth.

"I know you are going through a lot because I've spoken to your parents but I want you to understand that we are doing our best to bring the perpetrator to justice" said Sgt. Pugg. "This is taking too long for such a small town" said Ruth. "Yes, I agree with that but it doesn't necessarily have to be someone from this town who did it, it could be somebody who was just passing through. Investigation will continue as long as an arrest is not made and you have my assurance that somebody is going to pay for this" said Sgt. Pugg. "I hope so because it would be grossly unfair if I am the only one who is going to suffer" said Ruth. "If you follow the history of police work, many criminals who committed crimes and think that they have gotten safe from the law because a long time passed ended up being surprised. Sometimes more than thirty years and they are still brought to justice, once the evidence is available so don't worry" said Sgt. Pugg. "Thirty years from now you might be retired," said Ruth. "Don't watch that If I retire or die the baton will be passed on to someone younger who will have access to the files which will be properly stored" said Sgt. Pugg. "Well, once God spare lives I'm going to hold you to your word Sgt. Pugg," said Ruth. "Thank you, you have my word" said Sgt. Pugg who ended her visit.

A few minutes after Sgt. Pugg left Ruth had an unexpected visit from Dorothy the lady who drove her to the police station after she was raped. When Dorothy entered the hospital room and saw Ruth sitting on the bed she said, "Hello, how's my little friend doing?" Ruth who was surprised to see her said, "Hi, not so good as you can see but

I'm trying to pull through," said Ruth. "I went to your home to look for you and saw your parents. Your mom told me what happened and where you were so I took the opportunity to come and visit" said Dorothy. "Thanks Dorothy, I really appreciate your visit because you were there for me from day one and I didn't even know you before the incident," said Ruth. "I want you to understand that you are my friend for life a matter of fact I'm old enough to be your mother so sit tight I'll always be there for you," said Dorothy. "Oh Dorothy that is so sweet to hear, when I look back at my life growing up God has been so good to me and you my friend is one of the good things. I think He was the one who spared my life during the ordeal and I give thanks to Him" said Ruth. "I'm not too sure about that may be because I don't believe in God but when I see a good person like you being hurt like this I have to ask where was God when you needed Him?" asked Dorothy. Ruth being very surprised when Dorothy said she doesn't believe in God asked, "You're an atheist?" "Yes and I've always been I cannot believe in what I can't see or touch" said Dorothy. "I grew up accepting and having faith in Christ Jesus the Messiah as the true and living God. What it means when you say there is no God is that you accept the evil conditions that surround you every day in life with no hope for you out of it. You have put yourself at the mercies of man who thinks he is in charge but he is not and the way of man will never get better without higher authority. The Holy Bible teaches me about Christ Jesus the Messiah and He is my hope without any question as the highest authority," said Ruth. Dorothy was very surprised to hear how strongly Ruth replied and said, "I grew up in a Christian home in England and saw my parents going to church every Sunday but when I saw how hard they worked and how poor they died I'm sorry I just can't believe in God anymore" said Dorothy. "One thing I can tell you, your parents are with Christ the Messiah right now being comforted," said Ruth. "I can bet you that if you dig up their graves you will find their bones still there" said Dorothy. "Yes I agree but their spirits were separated from the body and is with the Lord," said Ruth. "You sound like you're going to be a preacher one day Ruth" said Dorothy. "If it's my calling then I will truly oblige but for now I will continue to be a child of God and take the word to those who need it because the way of Christ Jesus the Messiah has never failed" said Ruth. "One thing I know we'll always be friends no matter what" said Dorothy. "That's true but we have to continue our discussion another time because right now you are disappointing your parents who taught you the way of Christ the Messiah" said Ruth. "OK we can talk another time," said Dorothy who said good bye and left.

While Dorothy was visiting Ruth at the hospital, Ruth's parents were at home having a discussion about her negligence. Ruth's mom was very concerned about dad's silence so she said to him, "I know how you are feeling but your silence is not doing the situation any good." "What do you expect me to say?" asked dad. "Our daughter is having a rough time and she's in the hospital so at least when we have a visitor please take part in the discussion" said mom. "You're still not telling me what am I to say" said dad. "Our daughter even tried to kill herself because of the pregnancy and on top of that the embarrassment she have to face she doesn't even want to go on the road afraid of what people are going to say" said mom. "You are the one who is always saying that I'm too hard on the children when all I tried to do was drill responsibility into them. This whole thing was because of her irresponsibility, first she refused to accept a drive home from church then she lost her medication and said nothing!" said dad. "So you're blaming me for this?" asked mom. "Let the cap fit where it fit because our children grew up seeing me as Mr. Hardman and you as the loving one who is always taking up for them when I'm trying to instill discipline. I love my children very much but I've noticed over the years that Ruth does not take life seriously and all I tried to do was to wake her up and let her be more responsible." said dad. "OK we prayed about it, what did Christ say we must do to solve the problem?" asked mom. "I already put it in His hands and leaving everything up to Him because no rapist is going to destroy my family. You know, I still don't think you are seeing the bigger picture because our daughter is carrying the rapist's baby but deep in my heart I can feel the victory that we're going to have over the evil one. As a Christian I am not going to condone murder, lie or involve in any form of cover up. She is going to have to carry the baby and when it is born it will be left up to her whether she want to keep it or not" said dad. "She said she is going to give it up for adoption and start college next year" said mom. "You see what I'm talking about you knew this all along and didn't say anything to me. When were you going to tell me?" said dad who stepped out of the room and slammed the door.

CHAPTER 9

RUTH CHANGES HER MIND ABOUT ADOPTION

Several months had passed with all of Ruth's schoolmates now in college studying in their various disciplines. It was not an easy thing to see but she had to now bare the harsh reality of life with the baby growing inside her day by day. Ruth was now in an advanced stage of pregnancy and any day the baby could be born. During her pregnancy she followed up on her scheduled appointments to the clinic not missing any because she realized that if she was going to have the baby they might as well both be healthy.

One Sunday morning Ruth was attending her regular Sunday Church service and she was very inspired with the message that morning. Everyone was in attendance so the message by the pastor had to be special. The pastor said, "We live in an evil corrupt world where man is in constant battle with the flesh and the devil is going around like a roaring lion devouring whosoever gets in his way. Brothers and sisters the Holy Bible teaches us that the way of Christ, the Messiah is our only hope and anyone who rejects His way is condemned. The choice will be yours as to where you will go, heaven or hell. You don't want it any easier than that so why are we still rejecting Christ way with all the proof that's in the Holy Bible? Christ the Messiah died on the cross and took away our sins and when He rose on the third day He appeared to His Disciples as proof that the grave could not hold Him. Brothers and sisters before He ascended to Heaven He left us with a promise that He has gone to prepare a place for Christians because what He had seen and experienced here in the flesh, this could never be our true home. Christ also assured Christians that one day He is going to come as the great Judge that was judged and crucified by man. Everyone is going to stand before Him and give account for their sins and when judgment is over He will take us to the place that He has prepared for Christians where we'll be with Him in eternal peace. No other so called god on earth had ever been rose from the dead or had ever promised their followers that they are gone to prepare a place for them.

Brothers and sisters let's just sit quietly close our eyes and visualize what heaven will truly be like. The fresh air and everlasting peace that we longed for will be there. Christ Jesus the Messiah will be the only boss. You will never get sick or grow old. There will be no more pain, grief nor sorrow. There will be no curse of poverty, no cantankerous landlord, no corrupt politician, no extortionist, no sexual harassment, no white collar thief, no unfaithful spouse, no more racism and all the days of your life you will be comforted. What a place! Just remember brothers and sisters, Christ Jesus the Messiah is the only way and He doesn't lie." After saying that the congregation said, "Amen!" and the service ended with a warm prayer by the pastor.

When the service ended and everyone was talking and greeting each other the pastor came to Ruth and said, "Can I have a word with you and your parents in my office please." "Sure," said Ruth. On her way to the office she called her mom and dad who walked with her. When they reached the office the pastor was seen sitting around his desk and he said, "Good morning again everybody please close the door and have a seat." "Good morning," they said and closed the door and sat down where they could speak in private. "You must be wondering why I invited you here this morning, well I'm going to be brief but first I must get your feedback. Ruth I found a Christian couple who is willing to adopt your baby. They are very nice people I know them for years and they have been trying for years to have one without success so they have my recommendation. The baby is about to be born any day now so what do you say?" said the pastor. Ruth hesitated and looked at her parents before she answered, "Pastor after feeling this baby kicking and growing inside me for so many months I've grown attached to the baby so I'm going to keep my baby. I'm not giving him/her up because this baby is an innocent being in the whole situation and I don't think I could live with my conscience if I give him/her up." "Very good this is a great act of forgiveness" said the pastor. "I'm not too sure about the forgiveness thing because if an arrest is made I'm going to press charges" said Ruth. "What you're doing here takes a lot of courage and I respect it because the Holy Bible which is God's word said you must love even your enemies so congratulations on your bold decision" said the pastor. "What are you going to name him/her?" asked dad. "The baby will have our surname if it is OK with you dad and mom I'll be depending on your support because I'm going to start college next year" said Ruth. "You know you can depend on us whatever decision you make because whether we like it or not it's our grandchild" said mom after dad nodded his approval in silence. "You have my full support too just make sure that he's raised in the way of Christ the Messiah from day one" said pastor. "That's a must" said Ruth. "Also I want you to look at the other side of the coin in your pregnancy the medication that you lost thus allowing this child to have life could work out to be a blessing in disguise. As a child of God just keep trusting in God and never cease to pray," said the pastor. "I will definitely do that because so far this baby has defeated all the odds" said Ruth and the meeting ended.

CHAPTER 10

RUTH HAS THE BABY

One night Ruth was at home watching television alone in the living room because her parents had already retired to bed. She suddenly started feeling contractions and what was worse, her water broke. Lucky for her, where she was sitting was not far from her parent's bedroom so she knocked hard and shouted, "Mom, dad help!" Ruth's parents got quickly out of bed and rushed to her rescue with her mom asking, "What's the matter, are you all right?" "My water broke!" said Ruth. "What, come on let's get her into the vehicle we have to get her to the hospital fast!" said mom. Right away her mom grabbed her suitcase which was already packed and dad helped Ruth into the vehicle.

Off they went full speed to the hospital and when they reached mom jumped out of the vehicle and ran inside. Shortly after the hospital staff was seen rushing out to the vehicle with a stretcher on wheel. They took over and put Ruth on the stretcher and rushed back inside the hospital to the baby delivery section with her parents tracking them. When they reached the delivery theatre Ruth parents were told to wait outside. Everything was happening so fast with mom saying to dad, "Looked like we made it in time." "Never thought I would have to go through this again this was the same identical way we had to rush you to the hospital to give birth to Ruth" said dad. "Yes, you're right and it was just about an hour apart" said mom. "I had my doubts in the beginning but this baby might be a blessing in disguise because when Ruth goes off to college we are going to be alone" said dad. "Hearing you speaking like this my prayers have been answered because in the beginning things were really on the low side you wouldn't even talk, thank you Jesus!" said mom. Dad held mom's hand as both of them sat in the waiting area chair.

Ruth's parents waited patiently in the waiting area for about forty minutes when suddenly they heard a baby cry out. "You heard that?" asked mom. "If it's who I think it is the baby is out, the only question now is if it's a he or she" said dad. About ten minutes after the doctor came out to them and said, "Congratulations your daughter just had a healthy baby boy." "Yes! I will have company soon to go fishing again because ever since Al left to serve in the navy I've not gone fishing" said dad. "So what happened girls don't go fishing too, I used to go fishing with my dad" said mom. "No it's a different vibe with a boy and why are you getting jealous because it's a boy?" said dad. Now that they know the delivery result and Ruth and the baby were resting in good care they went back home to return in the morning.

When Ruth's parents returned in the morning to visit her they saw her breast feeding the baby. "Hi mom and dad," said Ruth when she saw them. "How are you feeling this morning knowing that you just came out of delivery?" asked mom. "Very sore but the doctor said I should be out in another two days" said Ruth. "You just take it easy and rest because most of the time your first delivery is the hardest" said mom. Dad looked at the baby and smiled and said, "One thing I know for sure the biological father is definitely a Caucasian." "Dad, please don't bring up anything about the past it's heartbreaking" said Ruth. "I'm sorry I was just joking" said dad. "This baby is a very beautiful baby" said mom. "Thanks mom" replied Ruth. "The word is out so you should soon have a lot of visitors. By the way, pastor said he wants to be the godfather" said dad. "I had him down as godfather since the time we had the meeting in his office and Julie will be his godmother, she said she promises to come and visit tomorrow" said Ruth. "I cannot stay long I have to get to work so I'll see you later" said dad and he left taking mom with him.

The next day Ruth was flooded with gift cards from a number of people some she didn't even know. Later that day Julie kept her word and visited Ruth at the hospital. When Julie entered the hospital room she hugged Ruth and said, "Ruth you made it after all you been through, thank God!" "The road was very rocky and the baby is finally here in excellent condition" said Ruth. Julie wanted to hold the baby but it wasn't safe for the baby because she was just coming from the street so she just stood and looked. "So how are you feeling after giving birth?" asked Julie. "I feel a little sore but my strength is fully restored. I have to be eating up a storm because your godson eats a lot" said Ruth. Both of them laughed because of what Ruth said. "He's cute I wish I could hold him" said Julie. "How's college going?" asked Ruth. "Exams are going to start next week and I'm in full preparation. It was very difficult for me to come and visit at this time but I had to come to see how you're doing so I can't stay long" said Julie. "I'm glad you came and it is a pleasure seeing you, thanks," said Ruth. They hugged each other and Julie left.

CHAPTER 11

UNCLE LEO SURPRISE VISITS

One month after the birth of the baby Ruth took him to church to be christened by the pastor. It was a large service that Sunday morning everyone was present including the Mayor and Sgt. Pugg who was now promoted to lieutenant. Ruth named the baby Mark after the apostle of Christ and made a vow that she would fully commit him to church. After the church service she received several gifts for the baby, some of the people she didn't even know but it did not matter she gave thanks and fully appreciated them.

One day Ruth was giving baby Mark his daily walk around the block, pushing him in his stroller when she was approached by a man who said, "Good day, my name is Rock Batson of ZQR television. Can I have a word with you please?" "Sure what's it about?" asked Ruth. "Your baby is the most famous baby in town, you know that" said the news reporter. "This town is a small town when compared to others and I know that nothing happens in this town that everyone doesn't know about so if you think my baby is famous I can't help it" said Ruth. "With your permission I would like to interview you for one of our special programs on television," said the news reporter. "No thank you I don't want to be that famous" said Ruth. "But this might help the real father to come forward" said the news reporter. "To do what, do a prison term? Because that is certainly what is going to happen to him!" said Ruth in an angry tone of voice. "Oh I'm sorry I didn't mean to offend you" said the news reporter. "Let me tell you something you don't seem as if you have a clue to what a girl goes through when she is raped. My whole life is set back one year and it's the grace of God why I'm standing here right now speaking to you. I think you should go and get some advice from a professional before you touch a sensitive topic" said Ruth who walked away from the news reporter.

After a few more weeks Ruth knows that there are only a few people she can thrust with her baby. She never let her baby out of her sight because the real father who she can't identify could be somewhere out there lurking waiting on his chance to take away the baby. Ruth also knows that although everyone was smiling with her not everyone was with her. She had heard some of the unkind gossips that were going around. The gossip that hurt most was when she heard one of her church friends named Candi, who she would never suspect would say things like that gossiping with someone else saying, "How could Ruth give birth to a baby like that she must be lying about being raped." Ruth couldn't help when she overheard the conversation so she went to her and said, "I heard what you just said, you're a heartless human being! How could you expect me to do something different from giving birth to this baby who is innocent and precious in the eyes of God. As a Christian if I had done something different I could not live with my conscience. I please God not man so I have nothing to be ashamed about!" Candi was so surprised when she found that Ruth was there and heard everything said, "Oh I'm so sorry Ruth I should not have said that." "It's OK you're not the only back stabber, every day I learn who my real friends are. I can live without friends like you" said Ruth who went home and locked the baby and herself in her room and cried.

It was now summer holiday break for Ruth's friends in college. Julie her best friend had just completed one year in college and the first persons she visited were Ruth and baby Mark who was her godson. When Julie saw Ruth she gave her a hug and said, "How is my godson? And how is your college preparation going because I can hardly wait to see you start!" "Mark is asleep and in good health. It's the first break I've gotten from morning he just wouldn't go to sleep. College preparation is very good I'm all set to start in the next few weeks when you will be starting your second year" said Ruth. "It is rough! It's a hard discipline life but knowing the type of person you are, I know you won't have a problem," said Julie. "You got that one right I'm fully motivated and can barely wait to start," said Ruth. "Good, what's the latest going on?" asked Julie. "The past few months have been the hardest in my entire life but I managed to pull through with thanks to my parents and all of you in church," said Ruth. "While in school I thought of you a lot, maybe that was the reason why things were so rough but thanks to God who answered our prayers" said Julie. "Julie, you're the only friend that I can trust because some of the things that's been said by the people in town about my incident is heartbreaking," said Ruth. They sat for a while and talked about almost everything because Julie and Ruth have been friends for a long time and they shared most things in common.

About fifteen minutes after Julie left Ruth was sitting on the verandah with her baby when a man who she didn't recognized drove up to the gate and asked her, "Good afternoon is Mr. and Mrs. Reid here?" "Good afternoon Mr. Reid isn't here but Mrs. Reid is. I'll go and get her" said Ruth. Ruth went inside the house and called her mom and when her mom came out and saw the man she said, "Leo is that you, what a surprise come on in!" said mom. While Leo was walking in from his car he said, "I told Sam that I was going to give him a surprise one of these days." Mom gave Leo a hug and said, "After all these years you haven't aged a bit you looking good, man you really taking care of yourself. Anyhow, this is our daughter Ruth and our grandson Mark. Ruth this is your father's older brother, your uncle Leo." "It's nice to finally meet one of dad's relatives" said Ruth and also gave her uncle Leo a hug. "The last time I saw you, you were this tall and Al who I heard is in the Navy I've not seen in quite a while" said Leo. Just when Leo finished making his statement Sam drove up looking at the car at the gate wondering who is blocking his gate.

When Sam walked in and saw Leo he was very surprised so he gave him a hug and said, "You're really a man of your word when you said you're going to surprise me one day. What strong breeze blew you out here?" "Ever since my wife Dianne died and all the children got married and moved out I'm all alone at the ranch so my plan is to visit somebody every month. This is your official visit" said Leo. "Well I'm a bit more fortunate than you when it comes to that because Ruth will be leaving soon for college and it will only be my wife and I with little Mark" said Sam. "I was telling mom some months ago that when I graduate from college I'm going to organize a family reunion because this family I understand is very big and we are scattered all over the place not knowing each other" said Ruth. "I am going to pray that God spares life for you to make that plan successful because this family seems to be drifting further and further apart" said Sam. "Make sure that you have a big venue and I'm definitely going to look forward to this" said Leo. "All this has happened to our family because of economic reasons. We had to go where we could find jobs to support our families," said Sam. "I am not going anywhere and if I had to live my life all over again I would not give up the simple country life because it is the best life. Young people today who grow up in the country migrate to the city "bling" life as soon as they become adults. I just don't know why they want to go and live where everyone is living on top of each other," said Leo. "You can stay as long as you want Leo, we'll be glad for your company" said mom.

"I'm just spending the weekend" said Leo. "Is dinner ready because I'm hungry and I know Leo must be hungry too?" asked Sam. "Dinner will be ready in a few minutes," said mom. While they were waiting for dinner to be ready they sat and talked about everything bringing each other up to date with everything.

After they finished eating dinner Ruth sat on the verandah with baby Mark looking out when Uncle Leo went and sat down beside her and said in a soft tone of voice, "How are you feeling today?" "Not too bad I am really glad that I can finally meet one of my father's relatives in person" replied Ruth. "I'm sorry to hear what had happened to you last year your father told me what happened in a letter." "I'm steadily getting over it but I would definitely love to see an arrest made to close the chapter" said Ruth. "One thing I remember my father always said, what is hidden from man cannot be hidden from God the perpetrator is going to pay one way or another" said Uncle Leo. "This baby is going to grow up not knowing his biological father but he won't be short of love" said Ruth. "When you start college don't let this incident hamper your studies because you have to focus" said Uncle Leo. "I know but I'm very determined right now and success is a must" said Ruth. "Good, anything at all you can always rely on me and you're always welcome to my ranch anytime" said Uncle Leo. "Thanks very much I'll keep that in mind" said Ruth.

CHAPTER 12

RUTH FINALLY STARTS COLLEGE

The long frustrating wait by Ruth to start college was finally over. The day before the start of school Ruth double checked everything she had already organized just to make sure there was no mistake. Ruth sat down and prayed and when she finished praying her mom came to her and asked, "Are you all set for tomorrow?" "Sure mom I'm very excited, I don't even think I can sleep tonight" said Ruth. "Good, I'm going to make your favorite meal for dinner" said mom. "Wow thanks mom I really appreciate that," said Ruth. "I want you to know that your father and I have very high expectations for you. Yes, we were disappointed that everything was delayed one year because of your incident but just bear in mind that nothing happens before time. I will take good care of Mark the same way I took care of you and your brother so just focus and don't worry about a thing while in college," said mom. "Thanks mom," said Ruth.

The next morning Ruth was up early. She ate her breakfast and walked to the bus stop with her parents carrying baby Mark. When the bus came Ruth hugged her parents and said, "Thanks for having confidence in me, you're the best parents any child would want. Have faith because I won't let you down," said Ruth and boarded the bus.

After driving several miles, the bus arrived at its destination on time which was the college campus. Without hesitation Ruth went to the registrar's office and received her schedule. She was escorted to her dormitory where she realized that she was going to share room with three other students. When Ruth went into the room the other three students were already there so she introduced herself and the first good news she got was that they were all Christians knowing each other for the first time. Ruth's roommates introduced themselves as Sonia, Dawn and Sharon. Ruth and her roommates chatted for a while trying to get to know each other more and what they realized was that they were from different places in Texas. About twenty minutes after she finished organizing herself Ruth and the other three students left for orientation. They were given a tour of the College Campus by a guide who on each stop at various points reminded them of the strict campus rules.

The next day Ruth went to her first class, she realized that apart of being in a higher learning institution she had to do a lot of research. The lecturers do not pamper you like the teachers in high school and her mind had to be shifted to a higher gear. Ruth and her roommates organized group study because they were doing the same course.

As time went by Ruth and her roommates started having more confidence in each other. During their group studies they would pray before and after. One evening after their group session, they sat down together and started opening up more to each other by having a girl to girl conversation. Sharon said, "I notice that none of you have said anything about a male friend, I heard that sometime parties are held on a weekend at various locations. Any of you planning on going to one if you are invited?" Obviously from what Sharon said the other roommates looked at her as the party girl when Dawn broke her silence and said, "I'm sorry I do not have a boyfriend and my father warned me that boyfriends and studies don't mix so after graduation I can think about that." Sonia in agreement with Dawn said, "I have a boyfriend at home who has also gone off to college elsewhere and we promise to write each other as often as possible so if I'm going to go to a party it has to be strictly with him." Everyone now looked at Ruth wanting to hear what she had to say. She said, "As long as I am here studying the only boyfriend I need is Christ Jesus the Messiah so parties are a no, no." "Amen well said I'm in total agreement with that too," said Dawn. Even though Ruth was beginning to have confidence in them she did not trust them enough to tell them fully about herself so from past experiences she kept her personal business out of the conversations. Sharon after hearing the answers from the other girls said, "Please don't get me wrong I do not have a boyfriend, it's just that I met someone on campus that I like and he was telling me about the parties. I did not tell him that I would go with him but if you girls are this serious then I will not do anything different from this group." "Sharon you are an adult, do not let because of us you don't go and enjoy yourself because if my boyfriend was here I would definitely go on dates," said Sonia. "I don't see anything wrong with a date because back home I've been to parties but I made sure I was in total control," said Dawn. It was now bedtime so Ruth and her roommates ended their conversation and retired to bed.

Meanwhile back at home Mark was beginning to crawl and was trying to stand up under the watchful eyes of his grandparents. Sometimes she would hold his hand and help him to step off. "Time really flies just the other day Mark was a little baby in my hands now he's trying to walk," said grandma. "We'll soon be able to go fishing," said grandpa jokingly. "Please, we still have a long way to go for that," said grandma. "Hold him right there let me get the camera and take his picture. I want to send it to his mom so she can see his progress," said grandpa. "That's a good idea, hurry!" said grandma. Grandpa took Mark's picture while he was standing and holding on to a chair and said, "The Lord has been good to us no matter how things get tough He has always given us the answers to our problems." "I agree with that, this baby is going to be something special, I can feel it," said grandma.

CHAPTER 13

RUTH GRADUATES FROM COLLEGE

The years of hard work and dedication passed by quickly and Ruth was making one of her regular visits back home just before her final exams and graduation from college. When she got home she saw her mom and Mark sitting on the verandah and Ruth said, "Hello what's up!" On seeing her Mark jumped up out of the chair he was sitting in and ran and greeted her with a hug saying, "Mom! You're not going to leave again are you?" Ruth's mom also gave her a hug and said, "This is the easy part because when you leave he is going to be very sad your dad and I have to work overtime to calm him down." "I know but there's nothing I can do about it. In a few weeks it will be all over and we can finally be together," said Ruth. "The older he gets it's the easier it will be and one day when it is his time to go to college he will definitely understand," said mom. "It's one of those things that a mother has to put up with and I'm so thankful that I have God bless supporting parents like you," said Ruth. "Guess who is here?" said mom. "I don't know is it someone that I know?" said Ruth. "Your brother is here on one of his rare visits. He's resting on the couch," said mom. "What I haven't seen him in years!" said Ruth.

When Ruth went into the living room and saw her brother dressed in his navy uniform lying on the couch resting she didn't want to disturb him. She shook him saying, "Al, Al wake up!" When Al woke up and saw Ruth he got up hugged her and said, "Ruth what a coincidence you are here too because I wasn't expecting to see you. How's College?" "College is great I'll be starting my final exams next week and graduation is just a few weeks after that," said Ruth. "Wow, I'm sorry I don't think I'll be able to attend. I might be somewhere in Asia because of the Vietnam War," said Al. "Anyway I'm sorry I woke you but my visit is very short and I've not seen you in years," said Ruth. "My visit is short too I'm leaving in the morning," said Al. "You look much bigger in size and all those muscles you seem to spend a lot of time in the gym," said Ruth. "Yes I have to because there's a war going on and I have to be in top physical shape. Remember while growing up we used to see dad as a hard man, well his discipline prepared me mentally for the navy I have him to thank," said Al. "I always thought he was too hard but I never knew I would live to see the day I would say this. If I had listened to him my incident would not have happened," said Ruth. "How are things going with that have any arrest been made?" asked Al. "None because I couldn't identify him he had on a mask and long sleeve shirt. The only thing I can remember was that he was wearing an expensive cologne and he was very strong with the knife pressing against my throat." said Ruth. "Dad wrote me a letter and told me what happened and I was very withdrawn and upset because of what happened, especially when I heard that you couldn't identify him. I know most of the guys in the area and with the slightest description I think I would have an idea of who it was," said Al. "The only thing we know so far from seeing Mark he was definitely a Caucasian and that alone is not sufficient. He should have a scar on his inner left thigh because I stabbed him with a piece of board but that too won't be sufficient because the investigating officer said the police can't go around telling every white male to drop their pants to look for a scar," said Ruth. "Yes I understand and it could also be someone who was just passing through town," said Al. "That's the same thing the investigating officer said but I'm still hopeful that one day there will be a breakthrough and an arrest can be made so I can close the chapter," said Ruth. "I can still see where God has been good to you, you still pushed ahead with your life because a lot of women who had your experience ended up in a psychiatric ward and never recovered. Your son is cute and he is growing up very nice. Has dad taken him fishing yet?" said Al jokingly. Ruth laughed and said, "What concerns me most is when Mark gets older and starts having his birthday parties he is going to start asking questions about his father I don't know what I'm going tell him so I'm going to have to put it in the hands of God because I don't want to lie." "That's true and I wish you all the best with that," said Al. It was time for Ruth to go so she said to Al, "Tell dad that I said hi when he comes home from work and everything will be over soon." "I'll do that and he's going to be very surprised when he comes home and sees me," said Al. They ended the conversation and she told everyone goodbye and also asked her mom, "Please tell Julie hi the time was short and most of it was spent with Al who I haven't seen in a very long time. I will let you know as soon as the graduation date is set." "Yes I will tell her when I see her Sunday in church," said mom. Then she hugged everyone and left.

Ruth travelled on the bus back to school and when she arrived, her three roommates were there doing group study. Ruth said, "How was everything when I was away?" "Everything was okay with nothing unusual," said Dawn. "I hope I'm not too late to join the study team," said Ruth. "No it's never too late because we are now on the final stretch," said Sonia. "We were just discussing and practicing the way prescriptions are written," said Sharon. They studied together for about three hours before they decided to take a break.

During the break Sharon asked, "Is everything okay Ruth? Because any chance you get you are heading home" "Please leave Ruth's business alone we are all adults so we do as we please," said Sonia. "Thank you Sonia but it's okay, I really miss my family and can barely go a week without seeing them," said Ruth who still managed to keep her secret intact that she was the only one who had a child. "If my boyfriend was visiting home from college I would definitely want to go home and see him," said Sonia. "It seems like you two are very serious has the big question been popped as yet?" said Dawn. "No but when it's popped the answer will be a big yes and you all will be invited," laughed Sonia. "Wish you all the best girl and I hope that I will be the one to catch the bride's bouquet at the wedding," said Sharon. Everyone laughed at what Sharon said. "I am praying for mister right to come along soon after graduation so that we can get married and live happily ever after," said Dawn. "Life is not a storybook ending you have to take it one step at a time and take time to know him," said Ruth. "Yes I agree we will all be qualified professionals so we should just pray and wait on God," said Sharon. "I'm getting hungry let's take a walk and find something to eat," said Dawn. They all left to a chicken joint on the college campus to get something to eat.

That night when Ruth was asleep she dreamt about the rape that she experienced. It felt so real in her dream that she felt as if it was actually happening so she jumped up out of her dream sweating and breathing very hard. When she sat up on the bed she saw that her other three roommates were still asleep and didn't notice anything so she sat quietly to herself and prayed. When she finished praying she felt calm again and started to remember what the psychiatrist at the hospital told her. The psychiatrist said, "The horror of the rape that you experienced is not going to suddenly disappear it is going to appear in your thoughts or dreams from time to time. When it happens just pray and with time to come it will eventually go away. Remember time heals wounds and after sometime yours will heal. Don't be fooled it will never disappear that's why some never recover from the sad ordeal. How you know that you're healed is when it appears to you and it doesn't affect you as it did before but your faith in God is going to play the biggest role in your recovery." Ruth felt so good after praying and remembering what the psychiatrist had said that she took out her Bible and read some verses which were very helpful for a stressful life. The Bible verses are:-

1) **Do not worry about tomorrow.** (Matthew 6 vs 25-34)

   Do not worry about anything. (Philippians 4 : 6)

2) **Be content in whatever situation you're in.** (Philippians 4 : 11)

The day of Ruth's graduation had finally come and all of her relatives and friends were present except her brother Al who was on navy duty in Asia. Ruth had the distinction of graduating with honors and was just out voted to be the valedictorian. Everything went well during the graduation ceremony and Ruth, because of her impressive performance was given two job offers. After the ceremony Ruth's dad hugged her and couldn't hold back the tears and joy. Ruth said jokingly, "Dad it's the first time after all these years I've seen a tough man like you cry." Her father just smiled at the comment. All of Ruth's college roommates and relatives introduced themselves to each other on the campus lawn. It was a happy introduction because after four years in college everyone would now know each other. The biggest surprise was when Ruth introduced her son Mark to her roommates. When Ruth took Mark to the group she said, "This is my son Mark." "What! Where in the world did you get such a handsome baby?" asked Dawn jokingly. "Ruth you were such an inspiration to us, why didn't you tell us about him?" asked Sharon. "Can I hold him?" asked Sonia. "Sure, I didn't mention anything about him because I was so focused. Now you know why I used to go home so often," said Ruth.

A special something happened during the get together on the campus lawn, Sonia's boyfriend who graduated from another college the week before bent down on one knee in front of Sonia and proposed to her in front of everyone. He said, "Sonia I waited patiently for so long for this moment that I think I should be renamed Job. We've known each other since high school and we're now graduating college with our degrees, honey I think we should wait no more. Will you marry me?" "Yes, Yes!" said Sonia. With everyone witnessing he slid the ring on her finger and then kissed her. Everyone cheered and the chancellor who also witnessed the proposal said in an announcement, "Ladies and gentlemen this is history this is the first time on record anything like this has ever happened on campus after a graduation ceremony, I wish you both the best." "Well Sharon you're going to get your chance to catch the bouquet," said Dawn who had a good laugh when she saw the expression on Sharon's face.

When Ruth and her parents were on their way home from the graduation mom said, "Did you feel comfortable introducing Mark to your college roommates after being silent about him for so long?" "No I felt a bit uncomfortable but how much longer should I have waited. I felt the time was now right because I love Mark so much and I'm not ashamed of him. What I felt badly about was the way he was conceived," said Ruth.

CHAPTER 14

MARK STARTS SCHOOL

With time going by so quickly and many waters flowing under the bridge Ruth now has her profession and had been invited to several job interviews. After careful consideration she finally made her selection which was about fifteen miles from where she lived. Ruth's selection as a pharmacist was based on job security so she settled to work for a Pharmacy which was apart of the biggest brand name pharmacy in the world.

The evening before Ruth started working her friend Julie came and visited her to congratulate her about her achievements. When Julie saw Ruth she said, "When are you going to start your new job?" "Tomorrow morning at 8 o'clock so I have to be in bed early," said Ruth. "Why did you choose this particular place when you had the opportunity to work somewhere nearer?" asked Julie. "I am of the opinion that not all that glitters is gold, so my bottom line was job security. I don't intend to be going from place to place seeking a job in the future so I chose this company because they have a solid base and a good international reputation," said Ruth. "Yes I can hear your college experience flowing from your thoughts," said Julie. "You've been working one year now at a forensic lab, how's the experience there?" asked Ruth. "As a lab technician it has been very educational but challenging, the human mind is always put to the test and the sky's the limit," said Julie. "As of today we might only have time to see each other on Sundays at church because I will have to work on Saturdays and some public holidays. I specially asked for Sundays off so I could acknowledge my Sabbath." "I am a bit more fortunate because I don't normally work on weekends and only on special occasions work is done on public holidays." said Julie. "I really want to take this time to tell you thanks for being there for me through the worst part of my life you had really being more than a friend, a sister who I didn't have because at one point I got so depressed that I wanted to end it all. Now because of Christ the Messiah, good friends and relatives that I could trust I am standing on solid grounds." said Ruth. "I didn't have a biological sister either so I always saw you as a sister who is much more than a friend. It was a pleasure being there for you," said Julie who hugged Ruth and left.

It was now time for Mark to start Elementary school so on the day of registration Ruth filled out the necessary forms and took them back to the school's office. When Ruth handed in the filled out forms to the clerk at the desk she looked at them and said, "I noticed that you have not filled in the father's name on the forms it's a requirement from day one." "I'd rather leave it blank for now," said Ruth. The clerk looked at Ruth in a funny way and asked, "You don't know your son's father's name?" "He had not been in our lives so it is best if his name is left out," said Ruth. The clerk gave Ruth an extra form and said, "Since your life is so complicated get this form filled out and signed by a notary public and bring it back as soon as possible." "Excuse me! What do you mean by complicated? I think you should mind your own business and do your job more professionally," said Ruth who took the form and left. Good for Ruth Mark's godfather and pastor of her Church was a notary so she had no problem in having it dealt with.

As the years rolled by, Mark was now nine years old and a trailblazer in school - his school work couldn't be better. He made Ruth very proud and all his teachers over the years spoke highly of him. Mark's favorite cartoon characters were **Crocodile Jerry & Pals** and at nights when he was tucked into bed Ruth would read him a story from the book **Christian Bedtime Stories by Anthony "Marsman" Brown**.

One night after Ruth had finished reading Mark a bedtime story, he asked, "Mom, where do babies come from?" Ruth opened her eyes wide when she heard the question now realizing how intelligent her son had become and thought carefully for a while before she answered and said, "That's a very interesting question, let me first tell you about a pot of gold. There's an old story that says a pot of gold is found at the end of a rainbow and babies are found at the foot of the cross. Well, a pot of gold will increase in value as the years go by but unlike the pot of gold babies who are God's prized possession is worth far more than gold and they will grow and inherit the Kingdom of God if they trust and obey God. Which one do you think is more valuable the pot of gold or the Kingdom of God?" "The Kingdom of God of course," said Mark. "So let's leave it at that for the time being," said Ruth.

One day when Mark was ten years old his grandfather Sam took him fishing by the lake. That time of the year was also bird hunting season so while they were by the lake fishing Mark asked, "If you are my grandpa who should I call dad because all the other students at school have a grandpa and dad different?" That's the type of question grandpa was hoping Mark would not ask so grandpa replied in puzzle form because he didn't want to lie, "One day when the dust is settled and the coast is clear you will know who to call dad." Mark stood silent and looked at grandpa for a few seconds trying to figure out what was just said but grandpa stood silent and said nothing more. Deep down inside grandpa knew that that question is going to be asked again when Mark grows older and he is praying that he doesn't have to be the one to answer it. While their lines were in the water they saw two men coming from the bushes with their rifles and two bags filled with dead birds which they shot down. Mark asked, "Are they going to eat all those birds, killing them must be fun grandpa?" "One thing I want you to learn killing should not be for fun. The only time you should kill is when you are attacked and your life is threatened or you are hungry and need food," said grandpa.

One Sunday when everyone was at church the pastor made a surprise announcement. He said, "Brothers and sisters I want to announce the engagement of Sean and Julie both of whom most of us knew since they were babies attending this church. I first knew about it this morning and it all took place last night so it's a big surprise to all of us, may the good Lord bless and keep them both." The church members went to Sean and Julie who were sitting together and gave them their warmest congratulations. When Ruth went to Julie she said, "You don't have to tell me I know I'm going to be the maid of honor. I was making myself fully prepared for the longest while and I was wondering why you guys were taking so long." "We just want to be sure because we don't want this marriage to fail," said Julie. "Congratulations girl, wow this is awesome news!" said Ruth who hugged both of them and left.

Three months after going through marriage counselling Sean and Julie tied the knot in church and became Mr. and Mrs. Samuels. The marriage was performed by the church pastor and witnessed by Ruth and Larry who was Sean's best friend. The reception was held on the church grounds with everyone who was invited attending and when the bride decided to throw her bouquet Ruth was the only unmarried female not in the lineup. When the wedding reception was over Sean and Julie left and went on a Caribbean cruise for their honeymoon.

One Sunday two months after the wedding everyone was in church and after the service when everyone was greeting each other Julie whispered something to Ruth. She said, "Ruth, guess what!" Ruth stared at her and said, "You got a promotion?" "No better than that, I'm pregnant!" said Julie. Ruth and Julie jumped for joy and everyone was wondering why they were jumping. Julie said, "Only you and Sean know so far or maybe Sean had also told his friends because he was jumping in the roof when he heard." "You don't have to tell anyone else because little by little it's going to start to show," said Ruth. "Before I forget there is something I want to ask you for the longest while, why didn't you line up with the others at the wedding to catch the bouquet?" asked Julie. "I don't know I'm just not ready for that sort of thing yet. I'm still having nightmares about my incident," said Ruth. "Ruth, you want to see a counsellor because it's twelve years now? It's time for you to let go and get on with your life," said Julie. "My incident was very painful and horrific the man took my virginity in the worst way and I couldn't even cry out because he had this big sharp knife at my throat. I'm not ready to have any relationship with any man right now," said Ruth. "I'm sorry to hear this but I didn't know you were still feeling the effects. We should talk more often because keeping it to yourself is not going to help," said Julie who gave her a hug.

When Mark was in high school everyone in his literature class was told by the teacher to bring a book that they had read featuring a teenage love story. The name of the book Mark took was titled **Converted by Love by Anthony "Marsman" Brown.** It's the story about a Muslim girl from Iran and a Christian boy from Canada who miraculously met while they were surfing the internet. They communicated through High school and College and when they graduated the boy flew to Iran to meet her in person. When they met in

Iran their love got even deeper and he did what most thought was the impossible by converting her to Christianity using methods which makes the book a must read. All the students in the class swapped the book that they took with another student in class and after reading they swapped again. That swapping continued until all the students in class read all the books that were presented. When the class finished reading they had a vote as to which book was the best and **Converted by Love** came out with the most votes.

CHAPTER 15

MARK STARTS COLLEGE

A s the years rolled by with all the ups and downs it was now Mark's turn to start medical school. He was so disciplined and impressive with his school work in high school that he was able to assist teachers with the lower grades. Ruth still not interested in marriage and had no more children and supported Mark all the way, while Julie who gave birth to a daughter named Klysteen was just about to start Elementary school.

Mark on his first day in medical school with Ruth accompanying him went straight to the administrative office to receive his folder with all the instructions. About an hour after Mark had his orientation which involved a guided tour of the campus. When Mark was shown his dorm room he had only one roommate who he was meeting for the first time. This was quite different from his mother's time in college where she had to share with three other girls. When he met his roommate Mark shook his hand and said, "My name is Mark." "My name is Brendt, I'm from Germany," said his roommate with a slight accent. "We're going to be roommates for years studying medicine so I'm going to be straight forward with you I like a clean surrounding," said Mark. "Good and I like a quiet atmosphere where I can concentrate and get more done," said Brendt. "You have a deal," said Mark who unpacked and got himself organized.

When Ruth left Mark at the college and headed back home she received a letter in the mail. She opened it and read it and felt very sad with what she read. She sat on her verandah thinking about what she read when Julie paid her a visit. When Julie saw Ruth she asked, "What's the matter why you're looking so sad Ruth?" "You remember Dorothy, right?" said Ruth. "The lady that helped you the night of your incident?" said Julie. "Yes that's her, well she had moved back to England to live with her niece and her niece wrote me this letter saying that Dorothy had died last month from cancer," said Ruth. "Are you going to go to England to attend the funeral?" asked Julie. "No she was already buried but Dorothy on her dying bed dictated this letter to her niece and asked her to send it to me," said Ruth. "She must have been in a bad way why she couldn't write the letter herself," said Julie.

Ruth read the letter to Julie and this is what it said, "Dear Ruth, I really missed you and I hope you have fully recovered from your incident because I saw where it had taken a serious toll on your life. I always remember the conversation we had at the hospital when I told you that I'm an atheist. Well, after lying here on death's bed and thinking about what you said and how my parents raised me, I finally accepted Christ Jesus the Messiah as my personal savior. I am not going to see you in this life again because by the time you receive this letter I'll be with my parents in heaven and I know we'll meet again one day in heaven. So until we meet again, you were really a good friend."

"You know, you have to be strong in this life because the devil has raged a serious war in the heart of humans and some surrender and do his will. In so doing some have rejected Christ the Messiah and only acknowledge Him when they are sick and feeling severe pain. Dorothy was lucky that she had the chance to repent and accept Christ the Messiah before she was taken out," said Julie. "After reading the letter I felt sad because Dorothy was such a nice person but deep down inside I'm feeling good to know that she finally made the right decision before it was too late," said Ruth.

After all was said and done Julie started to tell Ruth what her visit was all about. Julie said, "There's a new system called DNA which was introduced to the legal world. This system can be used to accurately tell who was the real perpetrator in a crime and very important who your real parents are." "Hold on, what are you saying, that can actually tell who raped me and who is Mark's biological father?" asked Ruth. "Yes the Supreme Court had accepted it because of its extreme accuracy. Also several people who were wrongfully accused and given long prison sentences in the past were released from prison because of DNA proof," said Julie. "How does it work?" asked Ruth. "To start I will have to swab Mark's mouth and get his DNA then I will keep it on the computer at the lab and match it with what we already have and with the new ones that will come into the system from time to time," said Julie. "Tell me more my sister because this is the best news I'm hearing since my incident," said Ruth. "We have to be very patient because there are millions of men out there and if Mark's biological father had already died we will never get a match," said Julie. "Julie I wish you all the best in what you're doing because the rape incident had tormented my life for so many years and I need to get closure," said Ruth. "I know how you feel so I'll do my very best," said Julie who told Ruth goodbye and left.

CHAPTER 16

INVITED TO HATE GROUP MEETING

One day Brendt was walking on the college campus when a man came up to him and gave him a flyer inviting him to a brotherhood meeting. The man told him that he could invite as many people as he wanted and introduced himself as Brother Charles. Brendt who believed in unity among all people was very curious as to what the meeting was all about. So he took the flyer to his dorm room and when he saw Mark he showed him and asked, "You know anything about this off campus meeting?" Mark looked at the flyer and said, "No do you have any idea what's it all about?" "No I thought you would know something since I'm from Germany," said Brendt. "Well since we're invited we can pay them a visit later because it sounds like a church group," said Mark. "Okay that will be good," said Brendt.

Later in the evening when they were taking a break from their studies Mark and Brendt got dressed and headed to the meeting. When they got to the meeting, which took about ten minutes on foot from the campus, they showed the man at the door the flyer as proof that they were invited and were welcomed inside the meeting hall. When they sat down they noticed that everyone was dressed in full white and two of the members standing on the platform had a big wooden cross in their hand. About five minutes after they sat down the meeting was about to start. One of the men who Mark thought was a pastor went up to the podium and asked everyone to rise. On standing every one stretched out their right hand and gave what looked like a Nazi salute. Mark and Brendt looked at each other because they were surprised at what they saw but at that point they couldn't risk trying to leave because it would draw suspicion that they are not with them. After the salute everyone sat down and the man at the podium introduced himself saying, "Greetings my brothers I am Don Buckridge the National Director of the KKK and I was given the mandate to guide you on the route of white supremacy in Texas. In spite of being outlawed by successive Governments we continue to grow and remain committed and strong. In order to continue to promote white supremacy we will have to make ourselves lawful again. To do that we need more of our members in the senate and in time to come one of us will be president of the United States where we can make powerful decisions like setting up barricades to keep out invaders. As your

Imperial Wizard I am going to lead the way where that is concerned by running for Senator next year and with your support no one can stop us. As I said earlier we are growing and if we're growing we have to remain militant. To all members there is a new rule implemented to keep the KKK pure and that is to do a DNA Heritage test to prove who your ancestors were. When you get the result of this test you must be more than ninety percent Caucasian less than that you cannot go forward with the KKK. I am going to lead the way where that is concerned by going to the lab tomorrow to get mine done and please I hope no one turns out like brother Zoki because when he was investigated we found that his grandmother was an African American. It didn't end well with him because he had an unfortunate accident shortly after that. Good night!" After the leader said good night he gave a Nazi salute and ended the meeting with a thunderous applause from members. When everyone started to move around Mark and Brendt quietly slipped out and made full speed back to the college campus.

That night Mark and Berndt laid in their beds and stared at the ceiling because they just couldn't find the words to describe what they just went through. It was as if they visited hell and returned, it was something that neither one of them had ever experienced in their entire life. While Mark was trying to come to grips with himself before his nightly devotion he remembered a poem his mom used to read to him when he was younger from the book titled **Christian Bedtime Stories**. It went like this:-

WHAT IS COLOR

THAT MAKE THE MIND SO SOUR

WHAT'S WITH THE HEART

THAT INSTEAD OF KINDNESS

PRACTICE WICKEDNESS AND
THINK ITS SMART

WHAT'S WITH THE EYE

THAT AFTER SEEING GOD'S THRUTH

STILL MAKE THE TONGUE LIE

WHAT'S WITH THE EAR

THAT AFTER HEARING GOD'S WORD

STILL DON'T CARE

WHAT'S WITH THE BRAIN

THAT STORES EMOTION

AND INSTEAD OF FORGIVING
HAVE A RUTHLESS AIM

WHAT'S WITH WEALTH

THAT SOME THINK

IT CAN REPLACE CHRIST DEATH

IN SPITE OF EVERYTHING

CHRIST IS STILL MERCIFUL AND FORGIVING

The following week Mark took the bus home to visit his mom. When he arrived home only his grandma was home at the time, grandpa had gone to visit his sick brother and his mom was at work. Grandma who was very happy to see him gave him a hug and said, "Mark what a surprise to see you, why didn't you call us to tell us you were coming? I'm sure your grandpa and mom would have been here and I would have prepared your favorite meal." "I got some free time so I decided to use it to visit the family and unfortunately I have to leave this evening," said Mark. "Oh that's a shame the only other person that might be around now is Julie, I saw her not too long," said grandma. "Well just give me a minute I'm going to run down by her house and say hi before my time is up," said Mark.

Off Mark went to Julie's house to say hi and when he reached her house he knocked on the door. When Julie opened the door and saw Mark she was very happy to see him so she gave him a hug and said, "How are you? Come on in." "I cannot stay long I have to get back to the campus this evening. Unfortunately only you and grandma are at home so my mom and grandpa will see me on my next visit," said Mark. "What a pity because you've grown up to be such a handsome man your mom is going to be very disappointed that she didn't see you but I'll talk to her," said Julie. "I want to ask you something since mom is not available, do you know anything about these people calling themselves the KKK?" asked Mark. Julie opened her eyes wide and said, "Why are you asking me about them?" "One of their members gave my roommate a flyer inviting him to a meeting a few blocks from the campus so he asked me about them. I didn't know a thing about them so I told him the only way to find out is to give them a visit and that we did. In our minds we were thinking that they were a church group, so while we were in the meeting their leader gave a Nazi salute and everybody responded. The leader spoke about white supremacy and the thing he said that disturbed me the most was when he said that one of their members had an unfortunate accident when they found that out that his grandmother was an African American," said Mark. "Let me tell you something you keep away from those people as far as possible because they are the worst hate group in modern times. You hear me, because if they ever knew who your mother is you might not have left there alive," said Julie. "This man even mentioned that he is going to run for senator, imagine if this man ever gets into Government, God help us," said Mark. "Unfortunately, there are more like him especially in the police force but from time to time when they show their colors they are dismissed," said Julie. "We were very surprised at what went on there and we have no intention of going back," said Mark. "I cannot speak for your roommate but I can tell you personally that you have no place there and I can't even mention something like this to your mother she would worry herself to death," said Julie. "You're the only one that I mentioned this to so let's keep it that way," said Mark. "No problem but I'll be checking on you," said Julie who gave Mark a hug as he left.

While Mark was walking on his way back to his grandma's to tell her goodbye he clearly understood more from what Julie had said. On his way he saw pastor who is his godfather driving his car by so he signaled to him and when pastor saw Mark signaling he pulled over and stopped. Mark ran up to the car and said, "How are you pastor? I haven't seen you in a good while" "Come on in and drive with me we have a lot of catching up to do," said pastor. Without hesitation Mark jumped in the pastor's car and they were on their way. "How long will you be staying?" asked the pastor. "I have until this evening so I just checked with Julie and I'm on my way back to grandma," said Mark. "I'm heading to the prison, every Wednesdays I go there and have prayer meetings with some of the inmates who are interested. You want to come with me? I won't be long" said pastor. "Sure, the experience will be good because I've never been in a prison before," said Mark. When they got to the prison they parked outside in the parking area and walked up to the main gate. When the prison guards saw them they opened the gate and one of them said, "Greetings pastor, whose soul are you going to save today for Christ?" The pastor smiled and said, "As many as I can because there's plenty of room in the Kingdom of God for everyone." The prison guard laughed and asked, "Who is this gentleman?" "This is Mark, my godson who is making the rounds with me today," said the pastor. They gave Mark a routine search before letting him in and told him to leave his wristwatch and wallet with them at the front. After that they were led to the regular meeting room on the prison building and when they got there the prisoners who normally took part in prayer meetings were already there waiting. The pastor said, "Greetings my brothers, this is Mark my godson who will pray with us today." One of the prisoners named

Ritchie in the prayer meeting said, "Pastor we have a bit of sad news, Tricky Billy won't be with us any longer he died night before last night from pneumonia and he wrote this poem he wanted to share with the group." When Mark heard the name he asked pastor, "Is that the same notorious Tricky Billy that used to make newspaper headlines?" "Yes, that's him," said the pastor. Ritchie gave pastor the letter with the poem and pastor opened it then read it aloud to everyone in the room. The letter said, "I was born a humble child grew up in Sunday school but as I grew older I allowed the devil to distract me out of a contented life with Christ the Messiah to a life of crime. All this started when I associated myself with the wrong friends who convinced me that the bling life was the way to go. I got greedy and famous feeling that I could defeat the odds of going to prison and here I am now living a life of regrets. I want to share this poem especially with every Afro American in the United States so they can wake up and don't make the same mistakes that I made in life.

POEM

WE ARE GOD'S CREATION

SO LET'S HAIL HIS AWESOME SUPERIORITY

WE LIVED OUR LIVES RECKLESSLY

**AND DIDN'T TRUST AND OBEY
GOD AS PRIORITY**

WE STOOPED TO THE LOWEST LEVEL

TRUE PERSEVERANCE

AND GAINED NOTHING BUT
NEGATIVE POPULARITY

WE LOST OUR SELF RESPECT

AND TAINTED OUR
HONOURABLE INTEGRITY

WE DESTROYED OUR PRIDE AND DIGNITY

AND BECAME OUTCASTS IN
A FED UP SOCIETY

WE CONTINUED TO BLUNDER NOT
LEARNING ANYTHING FROM THE PAST

AND WOULDN'T STAND UP TO
OUR RESPONSIBILITY

WE FOOLED OURSELVES THINKING THAT
CHRIST IS NOT THE REAL BIG MAN

AND PAID SCANT REGARD FOR
HIS MAJESTIC AUTHORITY

WE FOCUSED ON WEALTH

AND ONLY CHRIST WORD CAN
BRING PROSPERITY

WE AFRO/AMERICAN FILL THE PRISONS

AND SADLY, WE ARE THE MINORITY

WE TURNED OUR BACKS ON EDUCATION

AND WASTED OUR GOD GIVEN ABILITY

**WE NEEDED TO BE MORE FORGIVING
BY STOP FIGHTING EACH OTHER**

AND END YEARS OF PAIN AND HOSTILITY

LET'S CONTINUE TO BE BROTHERS IN CHRIST

AND SERVE HIM IN SOLIDARITY

ONE LOVE, MY BROTHERS!

While driving on their way from the prison Mark said, "That poem from Tricky Billy is deep I will always remember it." "It's a desperate voice of a soul crying out for forgiveness in the wilderness" said pastor. "I definitely have to share it with my friends at the College" said Mark. When they reached Mark grandma's house pastor said, "Please don't take forever to visit me again." "When I visit again I'll definitely come and check you, good bye" said Mark. His visiting time expired so Mark just went in the house grabbed his bag and kissed grandma goodbye and went to the bus top back to the College.

CHAPTER 17

MARK ASKS ABOUT BIOLOGICAL FATHER

As the years rolled by Mark was on summer break and about to start his final year in medical school. Ruth who was on her day off from work decided to take a little walk by the lake with Mark so that they could discuss upcoming plans. While they were sitting on a bench by the lake having their discussion Mark who had a burning question he wanted to ask his mother for years ceased the opportunity and said, "Mom there is something I have wanted to know for the longest while and with all due respect I'm asking you to give me a straight forward answer because I am now an adult." "I think I know what you're going to ask but anyhow go ahead," said Ruth. "Mom, while growing up and seeing all my friends at school having a biological father I always wondered to myself, who or where is my biological father? When I ask grandpa he answers in a riddle and when I ask grandma she said I must sit and talk with you privately. Let me have it mom because I suspect that it's something bad why his name is not even on my birth certificate." Ruth took a while before she responded and said, "It's a long story Mark." "I have all the time in the world and I'm in no hurry," said Mark. "Ok Mark just listen and don't interrupt me until I'm finished," said Ruth. "No problem mom my lips are sealed," said Mark.

"It was in the summer of 1968 two weeks after I graduated from high school and waiting for an answer as to which college I was going to attend. One Thursday night after choir practice at church I turned down a ride and decided to walk home alone. While walking past an old abandoned building which has been torn down now, a man fully dressed with a mask grabbed me from behind and put a big sharp knife at my throat and threatened to kill me. I kept silent because I didn't want him to kill me so he pulled me into the old abandoned building threw me on the floor and raped me. I felt so bitter and embarrassed about the ordeal that I lost all hope of living and got desperate. I grabbed a piece of board which was lying beside me on the floor and stabbed him on his left inner thigh. He let go of me and that was when I made my escape. A woman that was passing by in her car saw me running and screaming stopped to help me then took me to the police station. A full report was made and the police called an ambulance which took me to the hospital after. I spent a few days in the hospital underwent a number of tests and luckily I didn't contract any STDs. It was too early to know if I was pregnant so when I was discharged the doctor gave me a little bottle of pills to take that would make sure

I would not be pregnant. When I reached home I couldn't find the bottle of pills but my period started and I was very happy thinking that I was not pregnant. I had my period at the usual time for four months then one day I started to feel sick. Mom took me to see a doctor and when he examined me he said I was four months pregnant. The doctor explained that it's a rare occurrence for something like that to happen. You're almost a doctor you should understand. I could not give a description of the rapist because he was fully covered and strong. The only thing I could remember was that he was wearing an expensive cologne. I went through some serious depression, I even tried to commit suicide especially when I saw Julie and my other friends starting college and I had to be at home pregnant. I was advised by some to give you up for adoption when you were born and criticized by some when I carried you. To be fair I even thought of aborting you but I prayed and good sense prevailed. After feeling you growing inside of me I couldn't give you up when you were born. My mom, dad and our church brothers and sisters helped me with you to the point that I could start college the following year. You will soon be a full doctor so you can understand certain things. The horror of the rape defeated me psychologically so I never had any interest of getting married and having any more children. The first clue we had about the rapist was when you were born, when we looked at you we realized that he must be Caucasian. So now you know it all, any more questions?" asked Ruth. Mark took a little while before he answered and said, "I'm sorry what happened to you mom if I had known it was like that I would not have asked and thank you for keeping me and giving me life." "Regardless of what the situation was I am and will always be your mother and I love you very much. When you graduate find yourself a nice decent wife and let me have some fine grandchildren," said Ruth who gave him a hug.

The next day when mom was at work Mark went and visited Julie who he understood was off for the day from work. When he reached the house he knocked on the door and Julie opened the door and welcomed him inside. Julie jokingly said, "What can I do for you Dr. Mark?" "Not yet, I still have one year to go," said Mark who laughed. "You want something to drink?" asked Julie. "Lemonade will be fine thank you," said Mark. "What area are you planning on specializing in?" asked Julie. "I haven't decided fully yet but it will either be the brain or the heart, I want to explore what drives the human body," said Mark. "That sounds good but don't try to play God," said Julie and handed him a glass of lemonade. "You should know me better than that," said Mark. "Make sure you give me your graduation date as soon as you get it because the entire church will be coming and a lot of elderly folks who have been here a long time will also be coming, some you don't even know but they know you," said Julie. "Wow, you guys make me feel important," said Mark. "Tell me something, have you encountered any of those KKK people you told me about some years ago," asked Julie. "No I've not gone back there but I read something in the newspaper that Don Buckridge their influential leader is now a senator," said Mark. "Then how did he become senator when the KKK is outlawed?" asked Julie. "The powers that be might not know he's the secret head of the KKK or maybe they know and keeping it hush," said Mark. "It's sad to see that man who is the devil's disciple making his way in the Government and who knows how many more like him are there," said Julie. "When I heard that man speak that night he was cold as ice," said Mark. "That's why I put my vote only in Christ Jesus the Messiah because I can't trust in man," said Julie. "Amen to that," said Mark.

CHAPTER 18

JULIE MAKES DNA DISCOVERY

As the months continue to roll by Ruth and her mom were at home preparing for Mark's twenty fifth birthday party, his final birthday celebration before graduation. As they were preparing grandma said, "I can't believe that it's been twenty five years already everything seems like he was just born yesterday." "Yes that's true but just remembering how it all started is still giving me nightmares," said Ruth. "By the way, what time are you expecting Mark?" asked grandma. "He should be here about six o'clock," said Ruth. "Good his cake in the oven and dinner should be finished on time," said grandma. Just as she finished saying that grandpa walked in sniffing and said, "What smells so good?" "It is Mark's birthday cake in the oven," said Ruth. "Who's going to cut the cake with him?" asked grandpa. "It will be his decision and he said he has a surprise for me so let's see," said Ruth. "Where are you going to put the presents?" asked grandpa. "On the table behind you," said grandma. "Remember to include his uncle Al's present too," said grandpa. "Yes we have everything organized and will soon be finished," said grandma. "I want you guys to know that everything that is happening here is all possible because of you," said Ruth. "It was our pleasure because it's the only grandchild that we know. Al said that he has a daughter in Asia but he is yet to bring her here and we would definitely love to meet her before we die," said grandpa. "How old is she now?" asked Ruth. "She should be about fifteen years old," said grandma. "Fifteen and none of us have ever met her! Al has to do better than that," said Ruth. "I think it's because he is so busy sailing around the world why he has not taken her as yet but he promised us to bring her this Christmas," said grandma. "Good I can hardly wait," said Ruth.

Later in the day about 5:30pm after the family finished their preparation for the small get together all the invited guests were there waiting on Mark to arrive. The invited guests were the church pastor with Julie and husband. They all played a very important part in Mark upcoming and only Ruth brother Al was unavoidably absent. While they were in the living room talking grandpa said, "I hope Mark is on time because I'm hungry." The pastor laughed and said, "At your age you better watch your weight so food should be the last thing on your mind." "Thank you pastor for those kind words of wisdom," said grandma. Just as grandma finished talking a car drove up to the gate. When Ruth looked outside to see who it was, she saw Mark and a female friend coming from the car. Ruth ran out to greet them and said, "You're just in time son and who may I say is this fine looking young Miss?" "Mom this is Mary she is my special friend," said Mark. "Ruth gave them a hug and said, "Come on let's get inside there are some people inside I'll love you to meet." When they reached inside Mark was greeted with a loud happy birthday shout from everyone and before they could go any further Ruth said, "This is Mark's special friend Mary. Mary, this is Julie, Mark's godmother and her husband Sean. Beside them is my mom and dad, over here is our church pastor, Mark's godfather." Everyone gave Mary a warm welcome and she said, "Thanks for such a nice welcome folks and may the good Lord bless you all in your endeavors." "I love the sound of that, which church do you attend?" asked pastor. "I attend Zion Baptist Church in Houston," said Mary. "Yes I know that church, is pastor Bob still there?" asked pastor. "Yes he is still our pastor," said Mary. "Pastor Bob and I go way back we attended theological college together so when you see him again tell him that pastor Charles say hello," said pastor. "I will," said Mary. "Let's save further talk for later because I'm sure Mark and his friend must be hungry. Come on let us go to the table now and eat," said grandpa. "I second that," said Sean. When they all sat around the dining table the pastor blessed the food and then they ate. "The food was delicious mom," said Mark. "Thank grandma she was the big chef," said Ruth. "Thanks grandma you made my day really special," said Mark. "Anything for you my grandson," said grandma.

After they finished eating and went back to sit in the

living room Ruth said, "What are you majoring in Mary?" "I graduated last year and I majored in Business Management and so far everything is good," said Mary. "Are you from a Hispanic background?" asked grandma. "Yes, I was born here but both my parents are from Venezuela," said Mary. "I want you to excuse the amount of questions we've been asking Mary but Mark is really special to us and we just want to know you better," said Julie. "I have one last question I would love to ask. How did you guys meet?" said Sean. "I love that question," said grandpa. Mark smiled and hesitated a bit before he answered, "I was at a friend's birthday party when I noticed this beautiful girl standing across the room from where I was. She was so beautiful that I felt as if I was hypnotized by her beauty which captivated my thoughts. I kept staring but she didn't look in my direction. Then suddenly she looked in my direction and our eyes got locked together. I smiled and she smiled back then the atmosphere felt like it was filled with magic, then like a flower pulling in the direction towards the early morning sun I felt myself in similar situation being pulled in her direction. I didn't feel my legs move but before knowing it I found myself standing directly in front of her. You all know that I'm normally shy but I had to get out of my shell so I said hi, my name is Mark and she immediately replied and said her name is Mary. That night we talked for hours and we found we couldn't have enough of each other company, the rest is history." "Wow! That was so romantic," said Sean and Julie.

"It's time for you to cut the cake then open your presents Mark because I think the food we ate has digested enough," said Ruth. When they gathered around the cake to everyone's delight, Mark asked Mary to cut the cake with him. Before the cutting the cake was blessed by the pastor and everyone expressed their well wishes for the future. About fifteen minutes after the cake cutting Mark opened all his presents and he loved every one of them and said, "I want to thank you all for everything not just now but from birth. You've been a real inspiration to me while growing up." "Are you going to stay for the night," asked Ruth. "No we have to get back this evening because we're in full preparation for graduation," said Mark. "I know it's about three hour drive so please drive carefully and call me as you reach," said Ruth. "We definitely will mom and I should know the graduation date next week," said Mark. After saying goodbye, Mark and Mary set off on their journey to the college in the car leaving Ruth very worried. About an hour after everybody left Ruth was sitting on the verandah alone waiting on Mark to call when grandpa came and sat beside her and said, "Come on in and get your rest remember you have work tomorrow." "I'm just going to lie down because I know I'm not going to sleep until I get that phone call from Mark," said Ruth who got up and retired to bed.

The next evening Julie called the house by telephone and when grandma answered the phone Julie said, "Good evening Is Ruth home as yet?" "Yes she's home," said grandma. "Tell her not to leave I'll be there shortly," said Julie and hung up. About fifteen minutes after Julie drove up to the house and saw Ruth sitting on the verandah. When Ruth saw Julie she asked, "What's going on, Is everything OK?" Julie sat down on the verandah beside Ruth and said, "You're not going to believe it I found out who is Mark's biological father!" "What! How!" said a very surprised Ruth. "Remember what I told you about DNA some years ago that it can tell you who your real parents are and if you're innocent or guilty of a crime. For years I've been matching Mark's DNA with other DNAs sample we have in the system and I've finally found a perfect match," said Julie. "Who is it?" asked Ruth. "It's a man by the name of Don Buckridge who is a senator in the state of Texas and it is rumored that he is also the secret leader of the KKK in Texas," said Julie. "Is it OK if I ask mom something?" "Sure go ahead," said Julie. "Mom could you come here please!" shouted an excited Ruth. When mom heard Ruth shouting she came rushing to the verandah and said, "Yes Ruth Is everything OK?" "Yes everything is OK I just wanted to ask you something urgently. Do you know any Buckridge family living anywhere in this town?" asked Ruth. "Sure the Buckridge family lives about twenty miles north from here and they have a son who is a senator now," said grandma. "You mean Senator Don Buckridge?" said Julie. "Yes that's him I remember them because I used to do domestic work for the family before you were born," said grandma. "Do you know if they still live up there?" asked Ruth. "I don't know because from the last time I did domestic work for them I've not been up there but what I do know is that they were very wealthy Caucasians," said grandma. "Thanks grandma you were a big help," said Ruth. "Why are you suddenly asking all those questions about the Buckridge family?" asked grandma. "Nothing we can tell you now but you'll soon know," said Julie. "OK I'm glad I could be any help," said grandma and went back in the house. "We have our man!" said Julie sounding very excited. "This is the best news I've heard in years. I have a phone number for Lieutenant Pugg who was the investigating officer. She is retired now but she said if I heard anything I must contact her so she can call the police for them to open back the investigation. I'm sure she is going to be surprised to hear that it is someone as big as this but I'm going to telephone her tomorrow evening when I get home from work and we'll see where it goes from there. I think she's going to want to talk to you also Julie and for now we have to keep all this just between us," said Ruth. "This is going to make international news headlines," said Julie. "Well he put me on the news headlines and I'm going to return the favor by putting him back," said Ruth.

CHAPTER 19

POLICE INVESTIGATION REOPENED

When you think what was done was forgotten sudden destruction looms when you least expect. The next evening when Ruth got home she telephoned retired Lieutenant Pugg just as she promised. When Ruth dialed her number it rang twice before someone answered and said, "Hello, good evening." "Good evening can I speak to Mrs. Pugg please," said Ruth. "Speaking," said Mrs. Pugg. "This is Ruth Reid I don't know if you remember me because it's been quite a while," said Ruth. "How are you? I've never forgotten you," said Mrs Pugg. "I think we've made a big breakthrough in my case because of the introduction of DNA," said Ruth. "OK what! I'm free right now, you want to come and check me now because this is a long time," said Mrs. Pugg. "You're at the same address you gave me?" asked Ruth. "Yes it has not changed," said Mrs. Pugg. "OK, I'm going to leave right now and it should take me about thirty minutes to get there," said Ruth.

Ruth did as she said and left immediately. On her way she stopped and picked up Julie who lived along the route. When they reached Mrs. Pugg residence Ruth rang the buzzer switch on the gate and Mrs. Pugg came out and invited them in. When they went into the house there was a plaque on the wall with inspiring words which drew Ruth's attention and it read.

IF WHAT WE LIVED FOR

AND FOUGHT FOR

WAS WORTH DYING FOR

LET'S BE GRATEFUL AND SHOWER IT WITH

PRAISE, LOVE, RESPECT

AND APPRECIATION

IT'S CALLED DEMOCRACY

The three of them sat in the living room and Mrs. Pugg said, "OK let's get to the bottom of it, just explain to me what you discovered." "First of all this is my friend Julie who works at the forensic lab and she was the one who got the match on the computer," said Ruth. "When DNA was introduced by the Supreme Court to be used in evidence in a case, I took Mark DNA and matched it with almost every sample we have on record. This process I had been doing for years until now we have a perfect match," said Julie. "From my experience with DNA it's extremely accurate, it doesn't lie. Ruth you said I'm going to be surprised when you tell me who it is, now tell me who was the culprit?" said Mrs. Pugg. "It is none other than Senator Don Buckridge who is rumored to be the secret head of the KKK," said Ruth. "What! I didn't like that man from day one he's the meanest nastiest person you never want to get in contact with, and imagine he's now in our government. I voted against him in the election but unfortunately there are those who think he will bring glory to them, well we are going to disappoint them. You know that this discovery is huge. It is going to be all over the international news and I am going to get on this immediately. In the meantime say nothing to anyone about this," said Mrs. Pugg.

Mrs. Pugg wasted no time because the next day she arranged a private meeting at the police station with woman Sgt. Veloz, Ruth, Julie and herself. Mrs. Pugg said, "I'm no longer in the police force so I cannot take it any further. However, this is Sgt. Veloz she will take over everything from here and reopen the case. I personally recommend her as the best person to continue and I will assist her in the best way that I can." Sgt. Veloz collected a statement from Julie and an additional statement from Ruth to go along with the one she gave twenty six years ago.

When Sgt. Veloz was finished taking the statements and completing the file she said, "All the samples taken at the crime scene twenty six years ago and your clothes which was collected at the hospital was securely stored as evidence by retired Lieutenant Pugg. Now without hesitation my next step is for me to arrange a meeting with the District Attorney as soon as possible. You can go home now but listen for a telephone call."

About three days after Ruth received a telephone call from Sgt. Veloz who said, "Hi, how are you? I finally got the meeting time with a very busy DA. Can both of you come by the police station tomorrow morning at 9 o'clock?" "That time will be OK, I'll pick up Julie on my way there," said Ruth. "OK everything is all set then," said Sgt. Veloz. Both Ruth and Julie even if they had something else planned this meeting will take precedent over everything.

The next morning when Ruth, Julie, Sgt. Veloz and the DA were locked in the DA's office to start the meeting the DA said, "I am Paula Segree the District Attorney and you must be Ruth and Julie." "Yes we are," said Ruth. "I have read the file Sgt. Veloz presented to me and I want to make something very clear, to get someone DNA that person must give it voluntarily or there must be a court order. Before we can go an inch further, please explain to me how you got it?" "I work by the lab and when DNA was introduced by the Supreme Court years ago I got a sample of Ruth's son's DNA and kept it on the computer over the years. During the years Heritage DNA came about where a person would come willingly to the lab and give their DNA so that we could determine which part of the world they are from. Senator Don Buckridge before he was Senator was one of the people who came to the lab voluntarily and got his mouth swabbed and his DNA taken. All DNA samples collected are kept on the computer so I matched Ruth's son's DNA with some of them and found a perfect match with Senator Don Buckridge. Before giving their DNA everybody signed a document that they gave it willingly and it would be kept on record," said Julie. "I want you to bring me that document showing the date and time that Senator Don Buckridge signed and the DNA match with Ruth's son and Senator Buckridge as soon as possible. By the way I just want to get something very clear to make sure we're on the same page, Ruth son that you mentioned was he the result of the rape?" asked the DA. "Yes he is," said Ruth. "Oh this is even sweeter than I thought!" said the DA. "Say what!" said Ruth in a surprised tone of voice. "Please accept my apology for that statement Ruth. I'll be here till 5 o'clock so if you can come before that time today it will be even better," said the DA. "Apology accepted. What you said I felt very surprised but I know that you meant well and this is the happiest I've been in twenty six years," said Ruth. "I'm heading to the lab now so I'll have everything on your desk as soon as I can," said Julie. "Good, promise me something can we keep this to ourselves till an arrest is made," said The DA. "You have our word," said Ruth.

Julie got all the documents the DA requested but she wasn't able to take them to the DA the same evening because of her work load at the lab. The next morning when Ruth and Julie arrived at the DA's office and handed the documents to the DA she said, "I've examined them and things are looking good. I don't want you two to leave as yet because I'm going to prepare Senator Buckridge's arrest warrant and have it signed by a judge as soon as one is available." "No problem we're in no hurry we'll just call our offices and tell them we will be running late," said Ruth.

After about fifteen minutes the DA's assistant called her and told her that one of the judges had taken a break to his chambers so she can quickly go and get the warrant signed. Usually the DA's assistant would be the one to get the warrant signed but due to the high ranking official that's going to be arrested she took it herself. When the DA reached the senior judge's chamber and saw him she said, "Good morning sir, could you please sign this arrest warrant." The judge looked at the warrant and asked, "Is this the Senator Don Buckridge we are going to arrest?" "Yes sir, for a rape he committed twenty six years ago before he was Senator," said the DA. "Do you have solid proof? Because I don't want it to look as if we're trying to embarrass him or waste his or the court's time," said the judge. "We have perfect DNA match sir," said the DA. "Well what are you waiting for go and get him!" said the judge.

The DA went back to her office and called Sgt. Veloz to her office. When the Sgt. Arrived shortly after the DA handed her the warrant and said, "Don't matter where he is arrest him!" Sgt. Veloz left with her team of police officers and went immediately to Senator Don Buckridge's office. When the Sgt. Left the DA said to Ruth and Julie who were sitting in her office, "They have gone to pick him up and bear in mind life won't be the same again for you two." "What do you mean by that?" asked Julie. "Due to the magnitude of this case and the type of person involved, the press is going to set up camp outside your house or your work place just to speak to you. How they are going to know where you live or work I don't know but they will never get any information from my office. When this happens its best if you don't say a word to them about this case because they're going to try to twist things and try the case in the media. You can go to your work now and listen out for a call from my office." "OK we'll do that," said Ruth.

CHAPTER 20

SENATOR ARRESTED AND CHARGED

After years of waiting patiently for the impossible to happen there was now light at the end of the tunnel, it was payback time. When Sgt. Veloz and her team arrived at Senator Buckridge's office his secretary who was sitting on the outside of his office said, "What can I do for you?" "Is Senator Don Buckridge in?" asked Sgt. Veloz. "Yes he's in but he cannot speak to you right now," said the secretary. "Thank you that's all I want to know," said Sgt. Veloz. When the police stepped past the secretary and was approaching the office door the secretary shouted, "You can't go in there!" Sgt. Veloz leading the police team opened the senator door and saw him sitting around his desk. Senator Buckridge who was surprised to see the officers barging into his office asked, "What's the meaning of this?" Sgt. Veloz showed the senator the arrest warrant and said, "You're under arrest for rape, you have the right to remain silent anything you say can be used against you." The police handcuffed the senator and when he was escorted out of his office he said to his secretary, "Would you please call my lawyer and inform him about this because I'm going to have their badges for this." He was taken to the police station and placed into custody.

Before the first day of court the DA held a briefing meeting in her office with Ruth and Julie. The DA said, "I don't know how much court experience any of you have but there are certain things you have to understand before you enter the courtroom. When you take the stands you will be under oath so you must tell the truth. Listen carefully to the questions and give direct answers only to what you're asked. Ask the court to repeat the question if you did not hear it clearly. The accused cannot deny having sexual contact with you Ruth because his DNA is on every bit of evidence that we have. So he's going to have a high profile lawyer to twist things and attack your reputation and trying to make you feel like the ground under your feet is disappearing. Ruth, you have to be strong no matter what is thrown at you and last but not least, if anyone threatens or even looks at you in a matter you don't like during this trial let the police know. Now ladies, do you have any questions?" "What can we do about the annoying press at our gates?" asked Julie. "As long as they don't come on your property or touch you there's nothing you can do," said the DA. "No one is going to break me down I've waited too long for this, thank you very much DA," said Ruth.

While Senator Don Buckridge was in police custody his

lawyer went to have a meeting with him. The lawyer said, "I've read my copy of the file and from the look of things it's very serious because your DNA is on everything. I want to know what happened from day one so I can plan the defense in this trial." Senator Don Buckridge in an act of desperation gave his untruthful explanation to his lawyer. He said, "The woman and I were very good friends. She told me that she would like to go to Harvard University and I told her that I have a contact there. We agreed to meet that night so she could give me her information and when we met the only payment she could give me was sex. Well we had sex and it wasn't the first time we had sex. What made her get upset that night was when I told her that my contact had resigned from Harvard. Then she told me that you mean I had been having sex with you for nothing and ran off. Now after so many years I'm accused of rape. That is my defense." "And that is the truth?" asked the lawyer. "The whole truth," said the senator. "If that's the truth it will be your words against hers, we just have to prove that she's lying," said the lawyer. "I have one other thing I would like to be straightened out, when they are selecting juries for the trial I don't want any Afro/American on the panel because of my reputation with the clan my goose will be cooked," said the senator. "I am not sure I'll be able to do anything about that but I'll do my best," said the lawyer. "Your best, come on you have to do better than that!" said the senator. "I'll definitely do what I can do but you must understand that some things are just bigger than me," said the lawyer. "Thank you council," said the senator and went back to his cell.

Later on in the evening when the sun was about to set Mark and his girlfriend Mary went for a drive in the hills of Texas. When they reached the top of the hill and stopped, the beauty of the sun setting was so magnificent that they had to alight from the car sat on the car trunk together and held hands while they looked. Mark said, "This spectacular sunset I'll drive many miles just to see. It reminds me of the first time I saw you how beautiful you looked standing across the room. At that time I wondered what would it take to win your heart, should I do this or should I say that. If you look way out, you will see the stars beginning to light up over the deep blue sea and if you listen keenly you'll hear the birds whistle that you and I are meant to be." "Oh Mark that was so sweet," said Mary. Mark who wasn't finished with his romantic words got up off the trunk bent down on one knee while still holding her hand and said, "We have been friends for a long time. And we've been disciplined and patient never stepping out of line. It's now time for us to make that giant step with Christ in mind. Mary will you marry me?" "You know what you're saying it means that we're going to spend the rest of our lives together but I couldn't want less. Yes!" said Mary. With that delightful answer Mark took the ring from his pocket and slid it on her finger and said, "This is the beginning of what Christ the Messiah have started. We will announce it officially to our parents at my graduation next week." Then they kissed in the beautiful sunset.

It was now time for the first day in court everyone was in attendance including Mark who sat beside his mother. During their wait for the judge to come and take his seat at the head of the Court Senator Buckridge stared at Mark the entire time trying to get his attention. Senator Buckridge sat beside his lawyer who waited patiently for the start of court to put in his first bail application and feeling confident that he would be successful. At the beginning of court proceedings everyone stood while the judge was introduced by the court officer and then sat after the judge took his seat. Senator Buckridge's lawyer was the first to start off the proceedings he said, "I would like to put in bail application for my client Senator Don Buckridge who is not a stranger to anyone and he is definitely not a flight risk." "Does the DA have any objection?" asked the judge. "Due to the high respectable office he holds we have no objection sir but would still love if he surrenders his travel documents," said the DA. "OK, bail is set at five million dollars and all travel documents must be surrendered," said the judge. "Thank you sir," said the lawyer.

While that was going on Ruth's mom sitting on her verandah at home saw a blue limousine motor car stopped at her gate. Alighting from the car was a surprised visitor she had not seen in over forty years. Ruth's mom with her eyes and mouth open welcomed the surprised visitor saying, "Mrs. Betty Buckridge, what a surprise. I've not seen you in over forty years since I last worked for your family come on in." "I wasn't sure if you had still lived here but I wanted to see you so badly that I had to give it a try," said Mrs. Betty Buckridge. "I'm the only one here now everyone else is out, what brought you here today?" asked Ruth mom. "I'm a very sick woman and I'm not too sure how much longer I have to live. I've heard everything that had happened between my son Don and your daughter and I would like to apologize for all the pain that my son has caused. My son is an outcast now from the family for what he has done to his own father and this to your daughter only add to it," said Mrs. Betty Buckridge. "What did he do to father Buckridge? He was such a good boss." asked Ruth's mom. "His father died from drowning and the entire family suspects Don for the death. He has also committed a lot of atrocities to other people with his KKK friends. I pray that your daughter is successful in putting him in prison where he belongs," said Mrs. Betty Buckridge. "You said you were sick, what kind of sickness do you have?" asked Ruth mom. "I have breast cancer and from doctor's report I'm lucky to be still alive," said Mrs. Betty Buckridge. "I'm really sorry to hear that," said Ruth mom. "I have one request I would love to make I would love to see my grandson," "His name is Mark. I am going to have to work on that because I have to speak to Ruth first and hear what she has to say," said Ruth mom. "Thanks very much and I really hope you accept my sincere apology," said Mrs. Betty Buckridge and left with her driver.

It was time for Mark's graduation from medical school and everyone was in attendance. The ceremony was one of the biggest in the history of the school and after the ceremony while everyone was taking pictures Mark and Mary came to Ruth and said, "We are engaged to be married." Mary showed Ruth the engagement ring on her finger and said, "We have not set a date for the wedding as yet but as soon as Mark starts working at the hospital we will." Ruth was so excited that she called Julie, Sean, Pastor Charles and her parents over and told them the news. When pastor heard he said, "This is the type of result you get when you trust and obey Christ the Messiah words, well done Mark." "Mary, have you told your parents yet?" asked Ruth. "Yes we just told them and they are over there celebrating," said Mary. "This celebration will continue on our way home because we came for the graduation but you gave us plenty more to celebrate Mark," said Ruth.

On their way home from the graduation they stopped at a fancy restaurant to have dinner. They got a table where everyone including Mary's parents could sit together and celebrate. Ruth said, "This is a special day so please don't watch the prices just order what you want because I'm paying." "OK, just let me have a menu sheet," said grandpa. "And the good thing mom you don't have to wash up when we're through," said Ruth. "That's more than a relief," said grandma. "Let me add to this announcement, I got a letter from Al saying that he will definitely be coming for Christmas and he will be taking his daughter Lorna with him so that's another celebration we have to plan," said grandpa. "How old is his daughter now?" asked pastor. "Almost sixteen years old and none of us had ever met her," said Ruth. "He has a very busy schedule in the navy sailing all over the world which he barely has any time for himself," said grandma. The food was served on the table and the blessing was done by Pastor Charles then they started to eat. "Since we are all here I got a visit from Mark's grandmother Mrs. Betty Buckridge last week apologizing for what her son Don did to you Ruth. She is very sick and she begged me to take Mark to see her before she dies. I told her it would be up to you Ruth," said grandma. "I remember you used to work for them years ago and to what I can remember I think it was when you got pregnant with Ruth you had to give up that job," said grandpa. "No such visit like that will be done till after the trial next month because I don't want to get too friendly while the case is going on. Mark you heard that," said Ruth. "I hear you loud and clear mom," said Mark with his mouth filled with food. "Which hospital will you be working Mark?" asked Sean. "The one closest to Mary," said Mark. "Excuse me, that far! Are you planning on disappearing on me already?" said Ruth. "I'll come and look for you every week mom," said Mark. "I don't think that will be possible with the long busy working hours that doctors have," said Ruth. "I think that working that far might work out like a blessing in disguise because of the upcoming trial," said pastor. "I think so too Ruth because things might get ugly and the farther Mark is will be the better," said Julie. "OK, that makes sense I'll go with it but you and Mary must not be in any hankie pankie till after the marriage," said Ruth who made everyone including Mary's parents laugh because of the comment. While they were sitting there talking Ruth asked one of the waiters to take some pictures with her camera because it was the first time both side of the family were getting together.

After the pictures were taken and they were now preparing to leave the restaurant Mary father Mr. Rodriguez said to Ruth, "Our children is getting married soon and we've not had a chance to sit and talk." "As soon as a date for the marriage is set we can set our date because we are the ones who will be doing the major work and everyone you see here will be in the meeting because they are all Mark's parent" said Ruth. "Our family is huge and everybody loves Mark so you know the wedding will be huge" said Mrs. Rodriguez. "Mark is all I've got so whatever we plan has to be special" said Ruth. "OK, we have each other's contact number so we'll talk soon. Congrats for raising such a wonderful son" said Mr. Rodriguez. "Thanks and goodbye for now" said Ruth.

CHAPTER 21

THE TRIAL OF THE CENTURY

There were three days to go before the trial began and Mark was on one of his weekly visits to his mother Ruth. Before he got to her house Mark stopped at a food chain store to get something to eat. On his way out just as he stepped through the door of the store he met eye to eye with Senator Don Buckridge who was on his way into the store. When the senator saw Mark he said, "How are you young man, what a coincidence?" "I'm OK Senator Buckridge," said Mark addressing him by his title showing respect. "Hold on a minute do you think I should be addressed more like, say dad?" asked Senator Buckridge. "Please don't go there, you should be repenting and asking God for forgiveness for your horrible sins or you will never enter the Kingdom of God," said Mark. "I thought that after giving birth to you, you would be more thankful and appreciative," said Senator

Buckridge. "You have a serious problem and only Christ the Messiah can solve it," said Mark. "I'm sorry to say but you are giving me advice on something that you could never inherit because your kind is cursed and can't enter the Kingdom of God so I don't know what you're talking about," said Senator Buckridge. "This conversation is finished," said Mark who jumped in his car and drove off.

Mark was very upset with what Senator Buckridge said so he decided to visit his godfather the pastor before stopping by his mom Ruth. When he stopped by the church and saw the pastor he said, "How are you today, I want to talk to you about an incident I encountered a short while ago." "No problem, come let's go and sit in my office," said the pastor. When they sat in the pastor office Mark explained to him who he saw and what was said and the pastor replied, "In the Holy Bible Blaspheme is recognized as the worst sin because there is no forgiveness when you curse God. To me racism is equally bad because when you deliberately deny or belittle God's creation because they don't look like you then you are denying God. For centuries people have suffered serious oppression because of their skin color while the Holy Bible (Romans Ch. 10 vs11-13) teaches us that we are all equal in the eyes of God. Our founding fathers must be turning in their graves when they see what is happening because this country was built on moral values. Most of the hate is coming from a very vocal minority who try to behave as if they speak for everyone and Senator Don Buckridge is one of their leaders who will soon fall in the same pit he is digging for someone else. Mark, if you look back in history and see what has happened to people who tried to promote hate they have always been stopped dead in their tracks by an unseen force which is mightier than the human race. I am sorry for what was said to you but Senator Buckridge has a serious problem. I am beginning to wonder if this man is possessed by a demon because of the things he says and does always on the wrong side of God. I think it would be best if nothing about this is said to either your mom or Julie because it might upset them and the trial is just around the corner." "It's OK I'll leave it right here," said Mark who went on his way.

Meanwhile all that was happening Ruth was at work filling prescriptions when someone slipped her a paper she believed to be a prescription and when she read it, it said, "If the salmon didn't swim upstream he would not be eaten by bears." When Ruth went to see who slipped her the note under the window the person disappeared. She immediately made a telephone call to Julie and when Julie answered she told her about the note and Julie explained to her an encounter she had at a fast food restaurant while she was at lunch. Julie said, "I was at a fast food restaurant during my lunch break when a well dressed man came and sat in front of me and said "Small World Big Trouble." I was wondering what he meant by that but now you tell me about that I'm adding up everything." "They are trying to intimidate us!" said Ruth. "Yes and I'm going to call Sgt. Veloz right now because I don't trust them," said Julie. When Ruth and Julie left work and went home they saw a police vehicle parked at their gates because of the report they made. Mark who was at the house when Ruth went home asked, "Mom is something wrong why a police vehicle is parked at the gate?" "Not really it's just a precautionary method because the trial is so near," said Ruth who hid what happened from him and neither Mark wanted her to know his experience either.

DAY 1

The long awaited trial date was finally here and everyone involved was present and ready. The court officer ordering everybody present to stand then introduced the judge on his entry. When the judge sat down the court officer opens the court proceedings then told everyone to sit.

The first order of business was to get a plea from Senator Don Buckridge and of course he pleaded Not Guilty. Then it was time for the final jury selection. Senator Buckridge's lawyer launched objection to all the Afro/American that was on the jury panel. The DA didn't have a problem with that but it was when the five Afro/American was replaced with three Caucasians and two Afro/Americans and Senator Buckridge's lawyer was still objecting to the two Afro/American the problem started.

DA	What is happening here your honor why is the council objecting to all Afro/Americans?
Lawyer	Your honor all I'm trying to do is get a fair trial for my client who is not loved by Afro/Americans.

Judge   In terms of fairness I will allow this last
              objection.

In the end the final two Afro/Americans were replaced by
two Caucasians which makes the jury selection all white.
Before they got started the judge spoke to the juror panel
about their responsibilities that justice must prevail no
matter what. They are now ready to start.

DA   Your honor I beg to call my first witness to
              the witness stand Ms. Ruth Reid

Ruth came forward to the stand and was sworn in by the
court officer.

DA   State your name and occupation please.

Ruth   My name is Ruth Reid and I'm a Pharmacist.

DA   In July 1968 you had an altercation with the
              defendant Senator Don Buckridge. I want
              you to slowly tell the court in details what
              happened that night.

Ruth   About 9pm I was walking home alone
              along Zong Lane from Church. This was
              after choir practice and when I reached the
              vicinity of an old abandoned building which
              is no longer there today, I felt someone
              grabbed me from behind by putting their
              hand over my mouth and holding a big

sharp knife at my throat. The person said, "One sound and you're dead." He pressed the knife hard against my throat and this made me fear for my life so I followed his instructions because he was very strong. He pulled me into the abandoned building and threw me to the dirty floor. He pulled off my underwear and lie on top of me. I wanted to scream but because the knife was so big and sharp I didn't take the chance. Then the unthinkable happened, he forced himself in me and raped me. All I could do was cry and lie motionless because of how hard he pressed the knife against my throat. I thought he was going to kill me so I got desperate and took up a piece of board lying beside me and stabbed him on the inner part of his left thigh. When he got the stab he released me and rolled to the side holding the place where I stabbed him. I ceased the opportunity and ran out of the building and down the road shouting for help when a woman who was unknown to me at the time stopped her car and told me to jump in. I told her what happened and she took me to the police station where I made a report to Sgt. Pugg who arranged for me to go to the hospital by ambulance.

DA   Could you at the time identify your attacker?

Ruth No, He was fully dressed with dark long sleeve shirt and he had on a mask. He spoke through the mask so his voice was always disguised. The only thing I remembered was that he was wearing an expensive cologne and I couldn't tell whether he was black, white or blue because he was fully covered.

DA How did you know about Senator Buckridge's involvement?

Ruth My friend Julie who works by the lab was the one who made the discovery by successfully matching my son's DNA with Senator Buckridge's DNA almost twenty-five years later.

DA No further questions Your Honor.

Judge Council do you wish to cross examine?

Lawyer Most certainly sir. The night in question when you were leaving church, weren't you offered a ride home?

Ruth What does that have to do with it?

Lawyer Will you please answer yes or no to the question!

Ruth Yes.

Lawyer And you refused?

Ruth	I didn't want my friend to go out of her way.
Judge	Please answer yes or no.
Ruth	Yes.
Lawyer	Thank you. Aren't you a person who more than ninety percent of the time dress mode is pants instead of a skirt outfit?
Ruth	Those days, yes.
Lawyer	Weren't you told by your parents not to take that route home alone at nights?
Ruth	It's the shortest route home.
Lawyer	A simple yes or no will do please.
Ruth	Yes.
Lawyer	Didn't you tell your friends that you would prefer to go to Harvard University.
Ruth	Yes.
Lawyer	Didn't my client Senator Buckridge tell you that he has a contact to get you into Harvard University and you promised to meet him that night.
Ruth	Senator Buckridge and I didn't have any conversation about anything because I didn't even know him!
Lawyer	I want to remind you that you're under oath.

DA	Objection your honor she answered the question.
Lawyer	All I want is the truth because my client is facing thirty years in prison. Somebody is lying.
Judge	I will allow it but be careful.
Lawyer	I'm putting it to you that you made arrangement to meet Senator Buckridge alone that night for him to grant you a favor.
Ruth	Are you getting off your head I didn't even know that man!
Lawyer	I am putting it to you that you and Senator Buckridge had several secret dates together.
DA	Objection Your Honor, when is the council going to get it that that Ruth did not know Senator Buckridge!
Judge	Will both councils approach the bench please!

When the councils approached the bench the judge whispered, "What's the meaning of this line of question. Do you have proof of your allegations?" "My client word Your Honor," said the lawyer. "The doctor's report state that Ruth had sex for the first time that night," said DA. "Your client's word council is not good enough so unless you have proof stop before you're held in contempt," said the judge who ordered them to continue on a better line.

Lawyer	Are you a regular church member?
Ruth	Yes I am.
Lawyer	Which means you're a forgiving Christian?
Ruth	Yes.
Lawyer	When you were discharged from the hospital, were you given medication to prevent you from getting pregnant?
Ruth	Yes sir.
Lawyer	Will you please tell the court what happened to the medication.
Ruth	When it was time for me to take the medication I couldn't find it.
Lawyer	Did you tell anyone that it was lost or tried to get a refill?
Ruth	No sir.
Lawyer	Why didn't you?
Ruth	That same day I couldn't find the medication my period came.
Lawyer	I am putting it to you that it was because you knew my client family was wealthy why the medication disappeared.
DA	Objection Your Honor!

Judge   Defense council, this is your last warning.

Lawyer   I am finding it strange that as a Christian, you still want to send your son's father to prison after all these years.

Ruth   After that dreadful night, my life became a living nightmare I couldn't eat properly, I couldn't sleep or wanted to communicate with anyone! After saying that Ruth broke down in tears.

Lawyer   No further question Your Honor.

DA   No further question Your Honor.

Judge   This court will take a fifteen minute break.

After the break the court resumed its sitting.

DA   The court would like to call Mrs. Julie Samuels to the witness stands please.

When Julie came to the witness stands she was sworn in by the Court Officer.

DA   State you name and occupation please.

Julie   My name is Julie Samuels and I am a supervisor at the Forensic lab.

DA   I want you to slowly explain in details how you made your DNA discovery.

Julie

After the Supreme Court passed DNA into law many people visited the lab voluntarily giving their DNA wanting us to find out where their ancestry came from. On August 26th 1994 about 10 am Mr. Don Buckridge who wasn't a senator as yet, visited the lab and voluntarily got his mouth swabbed thus giving his DNA. He signed a document like everyone else giving permission for his DNA to be kept on record and can be used by the Police for criminal investigation. Mr. Don Buckridge wanted to prove to members of the KKK that he is a worthy white supremacist leader because his bloodline is more than ninety percent white. One day while matching DNA samples I was matching Ruth son Mark DNA with some of the DNA on the computer. This practice I had been doing since the Supreme Court passed DNA into law several years ago. While doing it I suddenly discovered a perfect match with Senator Don Buckridge DNA. I immediately contacted Ruth and the police because a twenty six year old crime which eluded the police was just solved. I had meetings with Lieutenant Pugg now retired, Sgt. Veloz, Ruth and the DA about the matter and the case was reopened and Senator Buckridge was arrested and charged for rape.

DA	No further questions Your Honor.
Lawyer	Does your work involve working with the police.
Julie	Yes sir, sometimes on weekends when I'm supposed to be off I have to report for emergency work with the police.
Lawyer	I understand that Ruth is your best friend, is that so?
Julie	Yes sir.
Lawyer	How long have both of you being friends?
Julie	A very long time, we grew up together sir.
Lawyer	Did Ruth have a boyfriend at the time of her alleged rape?
Julie	Not that I know of sir.
Lawyer	Your answer sounds as if you're not sure?
Julie	I would say no because if she did I would know.
Lawyer	Now let's get down to serious business. Weren't you the one who offered Ruth a ride home from Church the night of the alleged rape?
Julie	Yes sir.
Lawyer	Why did she refuse to take the ride home?

Julie	Ruth is a very independent person she has a mind of her own.
Lawyer	How long have you known Senator Buckridge?
Julie	Since he became senator but not to talk to.
Lawyer	Have you ever seen Ruth with Senator Buckridge?
Julie	No sir.
Lawyer	No further question Your Honor.
Judge	DA, do you have any further questions?
DA	No sir.
Judge	OK mam, you may step down. Call the next witness please.
DA	The Court would like to call Sgt. Veloz to the witness stand.

When Sgt. Veloz took the witness stand she swore in herself.

DA	State your name and rank please.
Sgt. Veloz	My name is Marie Veloz Sergeant of police.
DA	Will you please tell the Court in detail about the arrest of Senator Buckridge.
Sgt. Veloz	On March 3rd. 1995 about 11am I received a telephone call from retired Lieutenant

Pugg who invited me to a meeting. When I went to the meeting with retired Lieutenant Pugg Ruth Reid and Julie Samuels were also there so it was the four of us. In the meeting retired Lieutenant Pugg gave me a briefing on the case because she was the investigating officer when it started. After the briefing retired Lieutenant Pugg said the case was now in my hands to open because she was no longer a cop and could go no further from there. I collected a statement from Mrs. Julie Samuels and an additional statement from Ruth Reid and reopened the case. After that I arranged a meeting with the DA where myself, Ruth Reid, Julie Samuels and the DA could sit down and discuss the matter. The DA asked for additional documents and they were presented to her the following morning. Later that same day the DA called me and gave me a signed arrest warrant to arrest Senator Buckridge. About 12pm the same day I went to Senator Buckridge's office and saw him. I showed him the arrest warrant and read him his rights then I handcuffed him. When we were leaving his office Senator Buckridge said, "I'm going to have your badges." He was taken to the police station charged for rape and placed into custody.

DA	I have no further questions Your Honor.
Lawyer	At what point did you show him the arrest warrant?
Sgt. Veloz	Immediately when I saw him sir.
Lawyer	Did you allow my client a telephone call?
Sgt. Veloz	Senator Buckridge instructed his secretary to call his lawyer and when we got to the police station you were already there sir.
Lawyer	No further questions Your Honor.
Judge	OK I don't think we should go any further for the day. Let us resume in the morning.
Court Officer	All rise! This Court is adjourned till 9am tomorrow morning.

When the DA left court and went to her office Senator Buckridge's lawyer went to see her immediately. When the DA saw him she said, "What can I do for you council?" "My client would like to plead guilty to the lesser charge of assault and do ten years," said Senator Buckridge lawyer. "No way, you had your chance at the beginning but instead you went into court and embarrassed the complainant and made her feel like she was the one who was the criminal," said the DA. "Why are you taking this case so personally?" asked Senator Buckridge's lawyer. "If I do that then I will be stabbing the complainant in the back. This rape ruined her life and she waited twenty six years for payback. In addition if it wasn't the invention of DNA your client would have gotten away scotch free with a horrendous crime," said the DA. "Her son became a medical doctor! What better gift could she ask for, doesn't that count?" said Senator Buckridge lawyer. "You're pathetic, get out of my office!" said the DA. Senator Buckridge's lawyer picked up his briefcase shook his head from side to side and slowly left the DA's office without saying another word.

DAY 2

The next morning everybody was bright and early for the continuation of the trial. When the court was about to start the court officer shouted, "All rise!" When everyone stood the judge made his entry and sat down. The court officer then announced the restart of court for the day and the proceedings began.

Judge   OK council you can go ahead and call the new witness that you have.

Lawyer   Court officer can you call Candi Gondar for me please.

The court officer went to the door and called Candi Gondar. When she entered the court room and Julie and Ruth saw who it was Ruth said to Julie, "I don't believe my eyes, where has she been all these years." "I didn't even know she was alive and by the way, what does she have to do with this?" asked Julie. Candi took the witness stand and was sworn in by the court officer.

Lawyer	Introduce yourself please.
Candi	My name is Candi Gondar I am a high school history teacher.
Lawyer	Thank you Candi. Do you know Ruth Reid?
Candi	Yes sir.
Lawyer	Where do you know her from?
Candi	We grew up together in the same Town and went to the same church here in Texas.
Lawyer	Do you remember anything about the night that it was alleged that Ruth was rape.
Candi	Yes sir.
Lawyer	I want you to slowly tell the court in details what you remember.
Candi	Ruth and I along with other members of the church were at choir practice. After choir practice everyone was in different groups conversing and I noticed something unusual about Ruth. She was dressed in a skirt outfit so I asked her if there was a special occasion on why she was not in her regular jeans pants outfit. I didn't mean anything when I asked

her that but instead she got very defensive and told me to mind my own business and walked away. I didn't say anything more to her that night but when we were all ready to go home I heard Ruth's best friend Julie offering her a lift home and Ruth turned it down and started her journey home on foot. Ruth was the only one who headed in her direction while the rest of us headed in the opposite direction. The next day I heard people saying that Ruth was raped on her way home the said night she left church. That's all I know.

Lawyer	Thank you Candi, no further questions your honor.
Judge	Would you like to cross examine the witness DA?
DA	Yes sir. When was the last time you saw Ruth?
Candi	About twenty years ago.
DA	Where have you been living all that time?
Candi	I've been living in New York.
DA	And after all these years you're going to show up to be a witness. What drove you to this?

Lawyer Objection Your Honor, all we want to establish is the truth!

Judge Yes I agree because the truth is very important.

DA I want to remind you that you are under oath. Who sponsored your plane ticket?

Lawyer I sponsored her plane ticket because I will go to any length for my client just to get the truth in this matter. Someone is not telling the truth and we have to get to the bottom of it.

DA No further question Your Honor.

Lawyer Your Honor I would like to move the motion to remove Dorothy Tindale's statement from the case because she is deceased and it won't be possible for me to cross examine her.

Judge OK we are going to take thirty minutes break and I will address that when we return.

The court officer ordered everyone to stand while the Judge made his exit to his chambers. During the break there were smiles in the defendant's camp because they felt that they struck what is most likely a victory. While everyone sat quietly in their seats waiting on the Court to resume its sitting the DA slipped out quietly and went quickly to the telephone. Who she called and what she discussed no one knew but what they all know was that she came back with a smile.

The thirty minutes was up and it was time for the court session to restart. The court officer ordered everyone in Court to stand when the judge was about to make his re-entry. When everyone stood up they sat down just after the judge sat in his seat.

Judge	The motion which was raised by the defense council just before the break will be granted due to sub section 345a of 1946. Deceased Dorothy Tindale's statement is ruled out because the defense council has the right to cross examination in this matter. However, Dr. Fisher who did the medical report twenty six years ago is also deceased but the medical report will still stand as evidence so let's proceed with what we have on hand. Defense council, do you have any more witness to call?
Lawyer	No sir, I'm ready for my closing argument.
Judge	DA, do you have any more witnesses to call?
DA	Yes sir, the prosecution has one last witness to call.

Everyone in the Courtroom was surprised and starting to look around to see who it was.

Lawyer   Is this a ploy to waste the Court time? I wasn't briefed about any other witness in this case Your Honor.

Just as the defense council finished addressing the court a lady walked in through the court door.

DA   Your Honor this is Carol Buckridge the prosecution's last witness.

Senator Don Buckridge sat with his eyes wide open and the look of an angry cobra on his face then he leaned over to his lawyer and had a short discussion in silence.

Lawyer   What's the meaning of this, why is she here, what does she have to do with this?

DA   The defense council produced a surprise witness, it is now fair for the prosecution to produce our last witness.

Judge   I will allow it. Take the witness stand please.

While Carol Buckridge was on her way to the witness stand there was a very loud shout from Senator Buckridge saying, "Traitor, traitor!"

Judge   One more outburst like that from you Senator Buckridge and you will be held in contempt of court. And council will you please control your client!

Lawyer   I'm very sorry Your Honor. I promise no more outbursts from my client.

Judge   Court officer please proceed to swear in the witness.

The court officer proceeded to swear the witness and they were ready to start.

DA   Will you please introduce yourself.

Carol   My name is Carol Buckridge, I'm a businesswoman.

DA   Do you remember anything about the night Ruth alleged that she was raped by your brother Senator Don Buckridge.

Carol   Yes I do.

DA   I want you to tell the court slowly in detail what you remember.

Carol   The night of the alleged rape I was at home downstairs in the living room watching television when I heard the kitchen door close. I went to see who it was because when my brother comes home late he normally enters through that door. When I entered the kitchen I saw my brother sitting on the floor holding his inner left thigh with blood on his pants. I ran over to help him and asked him what happened. He told me that he was climbing a fence and slipped. When he slipped a piece of sharp board on the fence cut him on the inner part of his left thigh. He was in extreme pain so I did not try to move him. I then ran and got some towels which I spread on the ground and put him to lie on them with his legs stretched out. I took off his pants so that I could take a look at the wound and when I did I saw pieces of splinter sticking out of the wound. I told him it would be best if I took him to the hospital and he said no so I got the first aid kit and used cotton with antiseptic to pull the splinters out. When I finished cleaning up the wound I dressed it to the best of my ability and he asked me to keep it between us not to tell anyone. I started to get suspicious when I read the newspaper two days later and saw where a girl was raped the same night he came in injured. She said that the attacker wore a mask with dark colored long sleeved clothes and she stabbed him with a piece of board on his left inner thigh. I remembered when I was taking the towels and the clothes he was wearing to put in the incinerator to be burned because they were covered in blood, I found a mask in his pants pocket. Being as it was he was my brother and I promised that I wouldn't say anything so I burned everything. I nursed him back to good health and no one suspected anything. I'm sorry I didn't come forward and made a report when it happened.

DA   No further questions Your Honor.

Judge   Do you wish to cross examine the witness council.

Lawyer   Why should the court now believe what you are saying after keeping silent for so many years?

Carol   Because I'm under oath sir. You heard my brother's outburst when I came in because he knew I know the truth.

Lawyer   What has your brother done to you so bad that you would try to disgrace him like this?

DA   Objection Your Honor. The defense clearly stated earlier that he would go to any length just to get the truth. The witness is under oath.

Judge   Sustain.

Lawyer	I'm putting it to you why you are now giving evidence it's because you blame your brother for the death of your father.
Carol	No such thing sir.
Lawyer	And I'm also putting it to you that once your brother is out of the way you will be the sole heir to your parent valuable estate.
Carol	I don't know about that because my mom is the only one that can make that decision and she might surprise us all.
Lawyer	Speaking of your mom how is her health?
Carol	She is not doing too well.
Lawyer	Speak up please so that the court can hear you clearly.
Carol	She has cancer!
Lawyer	No further questions Your Honor.
Judge	The witness may step down. Is there any more surprise witnesses?
DA	No Your Honor.
Judge	Now that all witnesses in the case have given their testimony I'm going to read Dr. Fisher's comment that he wrote in his report twenty six years ago. "I examined Ruth Reid on July 3rd. 1968 and found abrasions on the walls of

her vagina caused by a dry erect penis. From examination she was penetrated for the first time and no STD. was contracted. Semen samples were taken and stored. There was also a cut on the front of her neck caused by a sharp instrument in the form of a knife. Dressing and medication prescribed."

The court will adjourn till 9 o'clock tomorrow morning and we will hear closing arguments from both councils.

Court officer   All rise.

Everyone stood up and the judge left the courtroom.

DAY 3

In what appears to be the final day of the trial everyone was early as usual and the courtroom was a jam packed. When the court was about to start the court officer shouted, "All rise!" When everyone stood up the judge entered the courtroom and took his seat at the head of proceedings. Then everyone followed by sitting down also.

Judge   Councils, Is there anything else to be added before you start your closing arguments?

DA   Nothing else Your Honor we are all ready to start our closing arguments.

Judge   OK, defense council you may begin.

In a jam packed silent courtroom, the lawyer got up from behind his desk and took three steps towards the center of the courtroom and began.

Lawyer   Your Honor, prosecution and members of the jury I'm not going to beat around the bush in my closing argument, I'm going to be as straight forward as I can. My client Senator Don Buckridge had sex with Ruth that night so that is not the issue whether they had sex or not. The real issue is, did both of them know each other and had sex with consent. Let's go step by step as I present the proof to you. That night in question when Ruth attended church everyone in church was surprised by the way she was dressed. Ruth wore a skirt outfit instead of her regular pants outfit and when her friend who testified earlier asked her if she had a special occasion after church, Ruth got defensive and told her to mind her own business then walked away. After church when everyone was about to leave Ruth was offered a lift home by her best friend and she surprisingly refused the lift even though it was late. When everyone was leaving Ruth again surprised everyone by going in a different direction from everyone else by herself. While on her way home, Ruth decided to walk on a lonely Lane which she was told not to walk on, whether if it was night or day. After all these surprising moves she is now going to chump up a rape allegation and said she didn't know who had sex with her. Well, Senator Buckridge in his statement stated that Ruth was his regular dating partner. Members of the jury someone is lying to the court! And things didn't end there, Ruth got pregnant because of sexual intercourse with Senator Buckridge because her medication which the doctor gave her to prevent the pregnancy mysteriously disappeared and when it did she told no one or tried to get a refill. Members of the jury Senator Buckridge was well known not only for football but his family is the wealthiest in this part of Texas so that is why the medication mysteriously disappeared. There's too much doubt in this case and because of that it boils down to Ruth's word against Senator Buckridge's word. Last but not least I am asking members of the jury to please ignore Senator Buckridge's sister testimony because she has no proof of what took place so her testimony should have no bearing on this case. Senator Buckridge and his sister are part of a family feud and she would do or say anything to get rid of him so please in the name of justice return a not guilty verdict in Senator Buckridge's favor. Thank you.

DA

Your Honor and members of the jury our founding fathers of this great nation fought and died for freedom and today we must cherish that freedom and never forget how it came about. Everybody in this great Nation has the right to wear what they want, walk where they please and say no to what they don't like. Ruth did that and she has paid a price for doing it. The defense is trying to convince you that Ruth and Senator Buckridge were friends and they have been on several dates. If Senator Buckridge was having sex that night with Ruth's consent, why did he hold a knife at her throat and why would she stab him? The scar from that wound is still present. All this, is just a chumped up story because Senator Buckridge is charged with a serious crime in which he will face time if you return a guilty verdict. Members of the jury your decision must be based on facts in which I'm going to remind you about. First, the doctor report stated that Ruth had sex for the first time that night when Senator Buckridge raped her so their story about going on several secret dates is false. Second, the same outfit Ruth described Senator Buckridge was wearing that night of the rape along with the mask was the same one Carol Buckridge described her brother was wearing when he came home injured the night after the rape. Carol Buckridge found the mask in Senator Buckridge pocket. Third, if you climbed a fence and got injured, what is there to hide? Senator Buckridge begged his sister Carol Buckridge not to say anything about the matter and she kept it a secret for twenty six years and when she turned up in court he got boisterous and called her a traitor which you all heard. The defense council in his closing statement said its Ruth's word against Senator Buckridge's word but the prosecution says It Senator Buckridge word against Ruth, Carol Buckridge and the doctor's report which makes it even more in favor of the prosecution. Members of the jury the defense is drowning and clutching at a straw so do the right thing by returning a guilty verdict. Then finally Senator Buckridge can be removed from his office and put where he truly belongs. Thank you.

Judge   Members of the jury, now that you have heard all arguments you may now go to your room and come back with a verdict.

The jury retired to sum up the case and the judge to his chambers while everyone waited patiently for them to return.

About an hour after the jury was ready with a verdict. The court officer ordered everyone waiting in court to rise when the judge was returning to his seat. Everyone was now settled.

Judge   Foreman of the juror, do you have a verdict?

Foreman   Yes sir.

The court officer took the paper with the verdict result from the foreman and gave it to the judge. The judge looked at it and handed it back to the court officer who immediately gave it back to the foreman for him to read the verdict aloud to the court.

Foreman   We the jury found the defendant, Senator Don Buckridge, guilty of rape.

After hearing the result the whole court except the defense council celebrated. The judge had to bring order in the court.

Judge   Senator Buckridge your bail is revoked and you will return on Friday for sentencing. Officers please take Senator Buckridge into custody.

While the court officers were handcuffing Senator Buckridge he shouted to the jurors, "You are all traitors, look at her! How could you take her word over mine?"

Judge   Get him out of my courtroom, he's a disgrace to his office!

Ruth, feeling more than relieved after a stressful trial, caught up to Carol Buckridge before she left and said, "Thank you very much for coming forward with the truth at a crucial time." "It's my pleasure because my brother and his KKK thugs have left a trail of destruction in Texas and it seems as if he always had support from the police. I vowed to stop him so I couldn't pass this opportunity to drive a nail in his coffin. Please I'm begging you one favor, my mom is on her dying bed take your son to see her as soon as you can because every day she asks for him." "I promised that I would take him to see her as soon as the trial is over. I'm going to telephone him and ask him to come as soon as he can," said Ruth. "So I'll see you soon," said Carol Buckridge. "Yes," said Ruth and both of them parted. While Ruth was on her way to her car she came face to face with Candi who said, "Ruth I want you to know that I'm sorry, please forgive me." "How could you have done something like that to me? I could have lost because of your testimony. We were church sisters before you moved to New York," said Ruth. "How is your son?" asked Candi. "He's fine he is now a medical doctor and will be getting married soon," said Ruth. "Your son is truly blessed I remember some of us were telling you to have an abortion or give him up for adoption when you were pregnant but you had faith and never gave him up," said Candi. "God has really been good to me, I forgive you but it's going to be very hard to forget what you did. Goodbye and have a good life in New York," said Ruth who jumped in her car and drove away.

It was now Friday morning three days after the guilty verdict. Ruth and her mom were sitting on the verandah at home waiting on a phone call from the DA who promised to call her as soon as Senator Don Buckridge was sentenced. Ruth's mom broke the silence and said, "You know, it's sad to see such a nice family like the Buckridges could have a son so wicked. His mom must be wondering what went wrong because he had loving parents and everything money could buy." "Maybe he was switched at the hospital after his mom gave birth because his sister was very caring and nothing like him," said Ruth. "No if that had happened they would know," said mom. "Were they Christians?" asked Ruth. "I don't know because I have not seen them in over forty years and when I was working there I didn't see any church activity," said mom. "That answers the question because children brought up outside the teachings of Christ Jesus the Messiah can be very unpredictable," said Ruth. Just after saying that her phone rang, Ruth said, "Hello." "How are you Ruth?" asked the DA on the phone. "I'm OK feeling a bit tired but what was the sentence?" said Ruth. "The judge sentenced Senator Buckridge to thirty years in prison and he must do twenty five years before he can be eligible for parole," said the DA on the phone. "That's wonderful news I also understand that he was stripped of the title of Senator while his entire family and coworkers abandoned him. Thank you for everything DA we'll keep in touch, goodbye," said Ruth and hung up her phone and got ready to go to work.

CHAPTER 22

MARK MEETS GRANDMA BUCKRIDGE

It was 10am the next morning which was Saturday and Ruth had her day off from work. It was a nice sunny day and the plan for the day was to take Mark to finally visit his ailing grandmother as soon as he arrived at the house. "What time did Mark say he'll be here Ruth?" asked Ruth mom. "He should be here already so I'm expecting him any minute now," said Ruth. "Make sure you call Mark's aunt Carol Buckridge and let her know when you'll be coming," said Ruth mom. "Yes as soon as Mark comes I'll call," said Ruth.

About fifteen minutes later, Mark and Mary drove up to the gate and when Ruth saw his car she said, "Thank God he's here safe." Mark and Mary alighted from the car and came into the house and greeted everyone. While greeting him, Ruth told Mark the wonderful news about the sentencing of Senator Buckridge and Mark was very delighted to hear because he always thought Senator Buckridge was too dangerous to hold a government office. Mark looked at his watch and said, "Are you ready to go and visit grandma Buckridge because remember Mary and I have to return this evening." "Yes we're all set but first we are going to stop by the church and meet Julie, Sean and Pastor because we're all going," said Ruth. "When they see us they might think it's an invasion," said Mark jokingly. "We are all one family in Christ and we've always done things together," said Ruth. Without any more hesitation they were on their way to the church, Mark and Mary travelled together in their car while Ruth travelled with her parents in her car.

When they got to the church, Sean, Julie and the pastor were ready and waiting. Without delay, the three of them went into Sean's car so all three cars set off on their journey. Ruth's car led the way because Ruth's mom was the only one who knew the way so she directed her along the way. After about twenty five minutes driving they finally reached their destination safely. When they drove up to the gate they dialed the intercom and when someone answered they identified themselves. After feeling satisfied who they were the person who answered the intercom opened the gate remotely. All three cars drove in and parked in the parking area. When they alighted from the car and saw the beautiful mansion Julie said to Ruth, "Mark's grandmother lives here?" "It's the first I'm coming here I didn't know the place was so beautiful and no wonder the police couldn't solve the case all those years. Senator Buckridge was here hiding behind all these riches where he was never suspected," said Ruth. "It has always been like this," said grandma. Just after saying that, the butler came outside to meet them and invited them inside. When they reached inside grandpa looked up in the ceiling and said, "Wow! The things money can buy." Just after saying that, Carol Buckridge came downstairs and greeted them warmly with hugs and handshakes. She stood in front of Mark and said, "You must be wondering why I'm looking at you like that, you're the spitting image of my dad your grandfather. How do you want me to address you, Dr. Mark or just Mark?" "Mark will be OK, thanks," said Mark. "OK everybody come, I won't delay any longer because my mom has gotten worse, it's a miracle she's still alive," said Carol who led them upstairs to her mom's room.

When they got to the room Mrs. Buckridge was seen lying on her back in bed with her doctor and lawyer sitting on a chair in the room. She said to them, "Come and hold my hand Mark because you're the most important figure here. I'm sorry for all of what your father did to your mom and I'm truly glad that I was able to meet you face to face before I die." "I'm truly glad to meet you too," said Mark while holding her hand. "I have only two children your father and Carol. You are the only child that your father produced because no woman wanted to be with him because of his wickedness. Carol unfortunately had no children because she was unable to. You are the only one who can carry on the Buckridge tradition and there were five traditions before you. Yesterday when I heard you were coming here I sat with my lawyer sitting on the chair behind you and willed over the entire Buckridge estate to you. Yes, you will be the new owner of the Buckridge estate when I die and the present value of it is eight hundred and fifty million dollars. Paintings and writings of the Buckridge tradition can be found in the library downstairs so you can read and learn about your ancestors. Please promise me something, it's the only favor I'm going to ask. Change your sir name to Buckridge, don't let your father's wickedness make you not want the name, the Buckridge tradition here in Texas is very respectable." "Yes Mark you have all of our blessing to do so," said Ruth. Mark looked at grandma Buckridge and said, "Yes I'll do that grandma and I'll proudly represent the Buckridges," "Are you married as yet or have any children?" asked grandma Buckridge who smiled when Mark called her grandma. "I have no children as yet but I'm engaged to this wonderful lady whose name is Mary Rodriguez. The date of the marriage will be set this week," said Mark. "Your fiancée is a beautiful woman Mark," said grandma Buckridge. "Thank you," said Mary. "Keep the wedding here because all the Buckridges got married right here on this beautiful property where kings, presidents and other world leaders visited," said grandma Buckridge. Right after saying that, she started to cough and choke with pain trying her best not to let go of Mark's hand until he could feel her grip loosening. Her doctor who was sitting in the room rushed to her assistant giving her oxygen and when her heart was checked there was no beat. Her doctor covered her face and said to Mark, "She is gone she put up a gallant fight and she got her final wish when she saw you Mark." Even though everyone except Ruth mom was meeting her for the first time sadness filled the air and tears could be seen coming from everyone's eyes as they stood silent in the room. The lawyer without hesitation opened his briefcase and handed Mark grandma Buckridge will and said, "You and I have to meet soon because you are the new director now." "OK, pastor I'm asking your help with this because I've never done anything like this before," said Mark. "Don't worry, you can depend on me," said pastor. "Mark turned to his mother and said, "I'm going to have to get some time off from work because my whole life has just changed with the blink of an eye." "Just make sure whatever you do Christ the Messiah is at the forefront of everything," said Ruth. Mark then turned to Mary and said, "I have to get my name sorted out before we get married, is that OK?" "Yes it's very important," said Mary. "Just leave that to me," said the family lawyer.

Later on the funeral parlor came and collected grandma Buckridge's body and took her to the funeral parlor. When the hearse left the compound, Carol Buckridge took Mark and everyone on a complete tour of the property introducing all the workers to Mark their new director. While on the tour Ruth dad said jokingly, "There's one thing I've not heard anyone said Mark will have to transfer to the nearest hospital to here and later take Mary with him." "You're so right I can hardly wait to see that," said Ruth.

Three months later Senator Don Buckridge was reported by the press to have committed suicide in prison and that didn't affect the vibes instead everyone seemed happier. Mark surname was changed to Buckridge and he got married to Mary the following week in what was a huge wedding. Even

Ruth's brother Al and his daughter Lorna were able to make it to the wedding and everyone finally got to know her. It was noted at the wedding also that when Mary the bride tossed the bouquet Ruth surprisingly joined the unmarried ladies to try and catch the bouquet a complete turnaround from how she felt throughout the years before.

About one year later Mary gave birth to a baby boy and his father named him Solomon. The surrounding atmosphere was filled with happiness and Mark and Mary applied and was successfully transferred to a nearer job location in the area. While Ruth now a grandmother, finally got closure and closed a long nightmare chapter.

THE END

CLOSING PRAYER

HEAVENLY FATHER YOU'VE
PROVEN ONCE AGAIN

THAT WHAT IS HIDDEN FROM MAN

CANNOT BE HIDDEN FROM YOU

GOOD WILL ALWAYS CONQUER EVIL

THE REIGN OF THE WICKED
WILL SURELY DISAPPEAR

THEY WHO PERSECUTE THE CHURCH

WILL ALL WITHER AWAY

WHEN WE TRUST AND OBEY YOUR WORD

WE WILL HAVE NOTHING TO FEAR

FOR YOU ARE A JUST GOD

A LOVING FORGIVING SAVOR

AND ONLY YOU CAN DESTROY
BOTH BODY AND SOUL

YOU HAVE ASSURED US

THAT YOU WILL NOT FORSAKE
YOUR CHILDREN

EVEN WHEN WE BLUNDER

AND CALL ON YOU FOR REDEMPTION

YOU STILL ANSWER OUR PRAYER

THANKS TO YOU ALWAYS

FOR MAKING WHAT SEEMS
IMPOSSIBLE, POSSIBLE

IN THE PRECIOUS NAME OF CHRIST
JESUS THE MESSIAH I PRAY

AMEN